RED: THE COLOR OF

FAILURE

"Is it better to love without life or live without love?"

CAROL THOMPSON

ISBN-13: 978-1721628544
ISBN-10: 1721628541
Cataloging – in-Publication Data

Thompson, Carol, 1971-
Red: the color of failure: / Carol Thompson.
p. cm.
ISBN 9781721628544
   1.   Romance. 2. Infertility. 3. Title
               Printed in the United States of America – 2018

Dedication

Dedicated to the one that makes my soul smile, Chad.

Thanks for this incredible journey.

Chapter 1

1995

She felt the familiar gush. She did her best to ignore it. "Please God, not again – not now." She squirmed in her seat, the seat that Spencer had so romantically arranged at a swanky restaurant, the one typically reserved only for their anniversary date. This was supposed to be a celebration dinner, a celebration well waited for, a celebration that had been on hold for over five years. No, she wasn't mistaken; she felt it again. "God, no. Please no." She wanted to just sit there and ignore it. Yes, that's what she would do, just pretend. That warm fluid bubbling just beneath her was all in her over exhausted, stressed out mind. Yes, the physical and emotional drain the five-year journey had been on both her and her husband must have just caught up with her. Hadn't she just been to the doctor today? Hadn't the twelve-week period passed just today? Hadn't Dr. Warren congratulated her this morning? *Ignore – Ignore - Ignore*

"Babe, you haven't touched your food" Spencer smirked. "You know you gotta eat. You deserve it. Now, take a bite out of that $40.00 steak. You look a million miles away. What are you thinking?"

Carmen pushed some asparagus around on her plate. Spencer noticed.

"Hmm Hmm?"

"Oh, I'm sorry, what did you say?"

He smiled with the dimpled grin that Carmen fell in love with over a decade ago.

"I just said, it's unbelievable. I can't believe this is finally happening!"

"Me either" she thought. "I can't believe this is happening either."

Oblivious to her thoughts, Spencer rambled on about God's timing and patience and his visions of he and his "son" throwing a football around in the yard or pushing his "little girl" on a tire swing from the old pecan tree. Spencer just sat back and resumed his contended peaceful smile. A smile that just about washed away all of Carmen's sanity.

"God, please, please, please" Carmen repeated in her head. Unable to disguise the dampness behind her eyes any longer, she asked to be excused to the powder room. She didn't know if she would make it before the floodgates opened on not just her eyes, but the biles of her stomach as well. The room began to spin, a unique grayish air added to the heaviness Carmen was feeling in her heart.

The short walk to the ladies' room proved robotic and long. Carmen forced the dizziness from her head by focusing on the destination. Although there were the normal twists and turns maneuvering around delivering waiters and waitresses and sounds of happy banter at booths, Carmen was inside the locked stall before she knew it. Standing inside, with her head pressed against the door, she offered a prayer for the zillionth time.

"Dear Lord – Please don't let it be what I think it is. Please don't let me have started. "Dear God – I know it's selfish, but I just want a baby, God. I'd be a good Mom – Spencer would be a good dad. Hear my heart, Lord."

Fighting the uncertainty or the inevitable, Carmen didn't know which; she slowly pulled down her pants and undergarments and sat on the impersonal, unfriendly, cold, hard "throne of disgrace."

There as the tears spilled over the dam was the evidence, the evidence that Carmen had somehow pissed God off.

RED – THE COLOR OF FAILURE

Chapter 2

1990

Carmen knew something was wrong way before her doctor ever officially told her. As uncomfortable as she was with her physical looks, she was made from strong stock – healthy as a horse, so they say, in all respects but reproduction. Somehow years of athleticism and abuse to her body had negated her ability to conceive. Her womb had betrayed her. *"Damn Womb!"* Now, she was waiting in a typically happy place observing happy "parents to be" rub their bellies while she waited for the news that she wasn't much of a woman compared to all of the other fertile Myrtles sitting in here. The internal argument that she was having with God just wasn't helping. *"Why does she deserve a baby, God? Look at her; she's only a teenager and already has one under foot"* *"and that girl, God, she barely looks as if she can afford to keep herself afloat. I mean for Heaven's sake, who shows up at the doctor's office in pajamas?"* *"Why don't they have separate waiting rooms for those that "can" and those that "cannot"?* Carmen's eyes were welling up, and she was just about to bolt

8

from the waiting area when the nursing attendant opened the door and called "Mrs. Simpkins". The way she announced her name, with an exaggerated "p" only confirmed that this nurse didn't know anything about her and that she didn't care that she couldn't produce a baby. That lady was probably daydreaming, dreading the time that she got off work and had to pick up her own rugrats from daycare. Carmen would have never dreaded that. The assistant then dutifully ushered Carmen to yet another room to wait and ordered her to strip down and put the gown on "open in the front".

As Carmen waited on the stirruped bed with her bare bottom ruffling the stark tissue paper and staring at the popcorn-looking tile on the ceiling, she thought about the journey that had finally brought her into see the doctor. It was only after Spencer's coaxing that she broke down and agreed to let the doctor tell her that she was barren. Barren – a word that describes her womb and her heart today. Empty, fruitless, and dry. Carmen knew her body. She knew that after months and years of not trying but not preventing and then of the time that they had seriously tried but never getting pregnant, that something was damaged. Sure, they had tried all of the home methods with no results. They had tried the rhythm method, the ovulation calendar, the upside-down method, a damn turkey baster as a matter of fact and had considered acupuncture. Spencer had even reluctantly agreed to have his "little soldiers" examined in a sterile environment only to appease his paranoid wife. Spencer became frustrated with the ovulation calendar posted on the bathroom mirror, but punctually performed when the time was ripe. Lovemaking became routine and distant, a means to an end, not a passionate exchange of love. Carmen argued and pleaded that it would once again regain its glory, but only after successful in the reproduction area. Carmen was definitely the instigator when it came to pursuing pregnancy. She had always been competitive, and dern it if she couldn't do what women across the world, across the ages, had done forever. She would get pregnant. What she didn't know at the time was that God must have had another plan. Carmen knew heartache, she thought. She knew what it was like to psychoanalyze her thoughts and behavior. She just knew that when she had a small craving for peanut butter that it was a baby. She knew that when her breasts started swelling that it was because they were beginning to produce milk. She talked herself into being pregnant every month for every year for many years. Every month, however, her body gave up her façade with its monthly visitor.

Crimson – the color of Betrayal.

Carmen was still reminiscing her misfortunes when the doctor appeared. After the brief and uncomfortable exchange of pleasantries with him and his white coat and Carmen in her birthday suit was over, Carmen stared at the ceiling and continued to question God while the doctor explored her desert of fruitlessness.

The examination, although unpleasant, had been long past due, and Carmen knew it. Deep inside, she didn't want to confront her failure as a woman. She had delayed this visit for as long as she possibly could. Now all that was left was the spoken diagnosis from the fertility specialist that one of her friends had recommended.

The doctor ordered Carmen to dress and wait for him to return to discuss the exam. Again, she pondered all of the diagnosis he may come up with. She would force herself not to cry if he said there would not be a baby in her future. Lost in thought, Carmen once again prayed for strength to handle the news.

With a gentle knock, Dr. Warren reentered the small exam room.

"Mrs. Simpkins, your condition is not unlike many others. You are still young, but your ovaries are all dried up." She knew it - dried up – No words could have been truer. Dried up. At 27, Carmen was dried up. Useless and dried up. Like a raisin. Barren and empty. Although the doctor continued explaining his findings, Carmen's mind wandered to oblivion. Oblivion was a place where she forced herself to think of other thoughts in order not to cry in front of others. She was a terrible crier. Her cries always resulted in an ugly eye swelling, snot producing hot mess.

When oblivion couldn't hold her attention any longer, she forced herself to listen again. Carmen regained complete focus when she heard the word, "impossible". At least it was clarity and finality. The young patient jumped to conclusions. "Ok then, guess that's that. If conceiving is out of the question, then I guess you are suggesting adoption? *"Spencer will never agree to that,"* she thought. *"He's already said as much"* "Is that what you mean doctor? That I am unable to get pregnant?" Carmen felt her voice crack as she vocalized her deepest worries to a stranger she had just met. She tried to force herself to visit oblivion again, but this was just too real, and it was too late. Tears slipped from her eyes.

"Mrs. Simpkins, I should have let you digest that information first. I think you misunderstood. I said highly unlikely but not impossible. With the help of fertility drugs, your chances are increased dramatically." There was a hesitation and slight pause before he continued. "But with that chance also comes the possibility of multiple births." The doctor used the plastic female model from his countertop to demonstrate the female reproductive system and how everything worked. Carmen tried to listen and pay attention, but somehow, she just had been given a lifeline, one that quite frankly she thought was not going to happen. She had come here thinking the doctor was going to confirm her worst suspicions. She had known that there was something wrong with her gynecological parts, but now getting news that medicine would cure her problem made butterflies dance in her stomach.

Her eyes actually danced for the first time in several months. The tears so easily developed earlier actually dissipated. Multiples like twins? Carmen relished the thought. She couldn't wait to tell her husband. There was a renewed hope. She even smiled when she walked back through the waiting room of expectant mommies.

With prescription in hand, Carmen bounced to the pharmacist and even though insurance wouldn't pay for the $150 per pill cost, Carmen paid and headed home with five yellow pills and ready for a night of forced romance. Maybe God had listened.

YELLOW – THE COLOR OF HOPE

Chapter 3

Surprised when he walked into the foyer from work, Spencer was greeted by his wife clad in a very sexy negligee. Carmen was beautiful inside and out, he thought. By no means was she a size two supermodel with an hourglass figure but she was perfect in his eyes. Her athletic build and messy hairdo had always turned Spencer's head. She had this small little dimple on her cheek when she smiled and a long fret line on her forehead when she was angry. When they first met, she was wearing a softball uniform, but he stared thinking how sexy cleats and a visor made her. She could bust out in tears at a drop of a hat. When she loved, she loved loyally and completely. She would go out of her way to pick up a stray dog in the middle of the road and usually brought it home. She spent time and money on her grandparents as they aged and just smiled every time they told the same story for the third time each visit. Her heart broke when both of them passed. She spent countless hours worrying about the plight of one of her students in her classroom and would fight fiercely for friends who were having problems. She was a go to person for family and others. Spencer didn't know how she carried the loads of so many people in her soul. He was positive that if the roles were reversed, he couldn't do it. Saying she had a heart of gold sounded cliché' Spencer knew, but he couldn't think of a better person to hold that honor. His current situation suddenly clicked back into his head and realization crept over him. Here she was. She was his. The negligee was new, he thought. The pink lacy top barely topped her perky nipples and invited him closer. Spencer inched closer to his beautiful half naked wife.

With a sly but knowing smile, he asked, "What's the candles for?"

No words could have better answered the question than the intimate and deep kiss Carmen landed on Spencer's lips. With arms wrapped around his neck, the couple began to sway to silence, no music, only the flickers of the candles and the flicker in their eyes. There was just a mature love that exhumed from them although they were still chronologically very young. There they stayed, long enough to feel the anticipation and desire but not quite long enough to act on it. The want and need burned sweetly in both their hearts and bodies. Moments froze in time.

"Welcome home," Carmen crooned.

"I'll leave and come back again if I get that kind of welcome home," he joked.

Carmen snickered. He always had a way to make her laugh. They had been each other's high school sweethearts. When they became serious, Spencer had made it a point to "not be serious." He goofed off and played jokes and cut up all the time. He once told her that whoever made it to their deathbed first was challenged to make the other laugh. That beauty failed with age, but laughter didn't. That conversation had always stuck in her head. She can recall the exact night they had that discussion. He wanted to love that's true. But what he wanted more was happiness, happiness that came with both love and companionship. What a poignant thought from such a person at that age. Although she just dismissed it back then, she had thought about that comment many times since. That's just the kind of relationship they had built.

Hand in hand, Carmen led Spencer to the dining room table where they had a candlelight dinner complete with wine, roasted prime rib, and brazen carrots – a meal completely out of line for a Thursday night. Conversation had never been forced between the two – they had always had the ability to laugh and communicate with and without words. They exchanged the normal banter about the day's routines. Spencer told her of the guys' practical jokes at work. He always said that on any given day, he was good for one or two laughs with the crew he worked with. He called their daily goofies as just "shits and giggles." Carmen told him about one of her students and his plight to learn multiplication and the silly rap songs they made up to help remember them.

Carmen spit and puffed into her hands trying to imitate her student's rapping abilities but couldn't finish due to Spencer mocking her. They laughed. Tonight, however, they both had other things on their mind unwilling to bring up. Although there were high stakes at hand, both were hesitant to approach the subject so heavy on their heart. When it was apparent that they were tiptoeing around the subject, Spencer broke the ice.

Spencer took a cleansing breath and began,

"So….. I'm assuming the news was good today?"

"And why would you think that?"

"Possibly because at the current moment I am sitting at

the dining room table with my beautiful wife who is only

wearing a see-through negligee, still too much material," he

added "and having a full course meal fit for a king. Please share,

my queen."

"Happily," she thought.

"We have good news, better news, and bad news. Which

do you want first?"

"The world sure had a way of throwing curves," Spencer thought.

All day long he had wanted to text Carmen or call, but it was all

he could do to stay strong for his highly emotional, on the brink

wife, when he himself wanted to just cry to God in despair. He

opted to wait until he got home to read her face, the face that he

loved deeply and would give anything to see happy and content,

content with motherhood. The two had been high school

sweethearts. They knew each other better than they in all rights should. Spencer helped the softball team in high school and the coach always made him catch for her number one pitcher. The two became inseparable. Carmen had talked about being a "mommy" from day one. Although both had a long-range plan while they dated, their conversations always ended up with "when we have kids" talk. Carmen deserved it. Starting a family had always been priority number one right after college graduation.

"Tell me the good news" Spencer asked.

"OK, the doctor said that there's a good chance that we will be able to get pregnant with the help of fertility pills." After Carmen explained the whole visit in every single minute detail and they were completely optimistic that there may in fact be a baby Spencer in the future, Spencer just sat back and grinned. This was not what he had expected earlier in the day. All that dread he had about calling her simply disappeared with this news.

"Well don't you want to know the better news?" Carmen prodded.

"I just thought that was the best news – no good news – no better news. What could be better?"

"OK, so it seems that this medicine will help us get pregnant, but the better news is that we might get a 2 for 1 deal."

"Meaning?" Spencer quizzed.

"Meaning, that these meds increase the possibility of multiple births."

"Multiples? As in 2?"

"Two *(hesitation)* or Three *(hesitation)* or even Four."

"What? Really? Seriously?" Spencer's face illustrated the range of emotions from non-belief to surprise to reality. Grinning like a Cheshire cat, Carmen watched as the delayed reaction on his face became transparent.

"Well, that is definitely better news. Us with triplets? Oh goodness, a ready-made family." Spencer jumped and hugged his wife as if they had already conceived. It was a hug full of relief and love.

There had never been a doubt. Spencer was a wonderful husband. He was patient and kind and encouraging. He was the type of husband that got out in the middle of the night to drive across town just to get Egg Drop Soup when Carmen had a mild cough. He was the type of husband that brought home wildflowers from the job site because he thought of his wife. Carmen knew he wouldn't be anything short of "father of the year" material.

"The dishes can wait," she said.

"I can't," Spencer joked.

Carmen led her stunningly handsome and rugged husband to the bedroom and kissed him passionately until the clothes dropped, the temperature rose, and love was made. Spencer never asked about the "bad news" Carmen mentioned that night. In fact, it didn't come up until several months later.

GREEN – THE COLOR OF LIFE

Chapter 4

"Carmen, I tried to use my credit card today and it was declined."

Carmen's heart dropped with Spencer's words. She froze in her tracks.

There it was, the declaration that Carmen had been dreading for months. The inevitable, the verdict, the admission of wrongdoing had come to light in this one sentence. Spencer waited for a response and slowly raised his eyebrows signaling his impatience for an answer. Carmen never liked the eyebrow raising thing.

"Yeah, about that. Money has been a little tight lately."

"A little tight? Carmen, money shouldn't be tight. We both have good jobs and very few bills – why is it tight?" Spencer posed unknowingly.

"We've just had a few more bills recently. I'm sorry. I will clear up some funds first thing Monday morning." Carmen all but danced around the root of the problem. She wasn't going there

unless forced to by Spencer's questioning.

"Carmen, that's not the point. The point is I needed gas,

and I rely on my card to pay for that gas. And, it wasn't there.

That's a problem. What bills have we added?" Spencer prodded.

The high-pitched tone he reached meant he was gaining

impatience for an answer. Spencer didn't have a temper.

Generally, he was calm and cool natured. But over the years,

Carmen learned that he didn't play when it came to money.

Growing up, Spencer had lived simply. He learned the value of a

hard day's work. Although he vowed he would take care of his

young bride even without a college education, he also vowed to

never live beyond their means. He secured a full-time job right

out of high school and proposed that same week. Although at the

time Carmen had not even finished her college degree in

teaching, Spencer promised they could make it. That promise

had enabled the two to live a life that was modest yet fulfilling

with only a small house mortgage and monthly bills.

They had now reached the point of no return. Carmen had never lied to Spencer and wasn't going to start now. The omission of information was not the same as lying. Carmen had just failed to mention that for one week of every month for well over a year, she had to use the credit card to pay for the "little yellow pills" and the bill was mounting. She never in a million years thought that it would have taken this long. Every time she charged the huge amount to her plastic, she reassured herself that it would all be ok once the pills worked. But now with bills totaling in the thousands, a declined credit card and an upset husband, there was nothing left to do but cry and fess up.

Spencer waited. And waited some more.

"I'm so sorry. I'm so sorry. The clomid pills are kind of expensive."

"Wait, you mean insurance doesn't pay for these pills? It's medicine. Why don't they pay for it?" He was sincerely baffled. The crease on his forehead gave his confusion away.

"They say it is not covered. I don't know. Maybe it's because it is experimental. I just know that it is our only way to get pregnant. So, it's necessary. I have to have them. I thought it would only be for a few months." Carmen's tears got heavier and heavier.

It was now Spencer's turn to storm. "Carmen, you know how I feel about bills. We have to pay the credit card off every month. If we can't afford it, then we don't buy it." Spencer proclaimed. "How much do we owe?" Carmen sat with her hands over her face not a word vocalized. Both knew no good came out of the silent answer. Spencer raised his voice for the second time of the night. "Carmen?"

Carmen just sobbed even harder. She knew Spencer would be furious. And she was right. When she pulled the credit card statement from the desk drawer and gave it to him, Spencer went into silence mode. That was worse than him screaming at her. It took a couple of minutes for Spencer to peruse the history and flip the pages of last month's statement. Carmen noticed his squinted eyebrows and the pinched lips, all the telltale signs of his anger. He stormed outside to his shop. That was generally his go to place when he needed to be alone. It was his thinking area.

An argument of silence had begun. Paralyzed with sadness and guilt, Carmen moped around the house inattentive to anything.

That night was beyond horrific. Neither one of them spoke but kept their thoughts to themselves. Carmen couldn't believe that Spencer didn't think a baby was worth the money she had been spending. Heck, lots of people borrow the money to adopt. Some have astronomical loans. Maybe not quite the same, but very similar, Carmen thought. Her disposition ran the gamut from scared to shame to right out anger. Spencer couldn't believe that Carmen had hid this from him. Hadn't they always confided in each other even when it was embarrassing or bad? Carmen was financially savvy. He just couldn't understand how she had accumulated such a debt and how she had done it without him knowing. He wasn't sure exactly how he felt but he did know that she should have told him from day one.

What Carmen had thought was an easy answer to a long-term prayer, proved to be yet another agonizing emotionally starving journey. To compact the infertility problem, now she had a husband that was not speaking to her and hadn't in three days. There had been days in their marriage where they argued. Generally, it was about Spencer not picking up after himself or Carmen not keeping up with the mileage before oil changes on her Jeep. For the most part, though, their arguments were trivial at best and easily solved with a joke or two and a seductive smile.

After four miserably long days, the yearning for both Spencer's forgiveness and approval got too much to bear. Carmen gave in. In all fairness, it was always her that succeeded in arguments. She loved Spencer with every fiber of her being. She hated when she felt that he was mad at her or disappointed. Never before, though, had she seen him this upset. Carmen wondered if the journey to parenthood was about to end. She knew it was all her fault. How could she have been so stupid? Carmen prayed silently while she approached her husband.

"Spencer, please forgive me. The struggle to get pregnant has been overwhelming, and I didn't tell you because I was afraid you would put a stop to it. I know how you feel about credit, and quite honestly, I knew this would happen. I should have discussed it with you, but I blatantly ignored that conversation from the get go. I'm so so sorry."

Spencer stared at Carmen, a stare that she just couldn't decipher. For the life of him, he just couldn't stay mad at her. He, probably to a lesser degree, understood the frustration and the time involved with starting their family. It felt like life was just on hold until they created a tiny being from both of their genes. Spencer continued to stare into Carmen's soul. He prayed his own prayer. *"Lord, allow me to forgive. Help me to help her."*

There were no words of forgiveness spoken, just a hug and a deep and intimate kiss. Life was right again. After all of the problems seeped through the loving embrace and seemed to dissipate into thin air, Spencer pulled away and looked into Carmen's eyes. "It's worth it, babe. We will be alright." Then he concluded with "and I've got some scheduled overtime this week to help start tackling these bills." That was all he had to say for his young wife to cry with shame, acceptance, love and complete awe of this man that she found so many years ago on the softball field in their little small hometown in Georgia. As he wiped away the tears from her eyes and smiled, Spencer said, "Now let's go work on that baby." Carmen seductively obliged.

GOLD – THE COLOR OF FORGIVENESS

Chapter 5

At work the next day, Carmen kept rewinding and playing the conversation and the lovemaking in her head from the night before. There had never been such tenderness in Spencer's touch. It felt as it did the first time, a need. The need was real. After fighting and arguing and all of the stress, Carmen just blocked the failures and faults from her mind and surrendered to the man she loved, the man she didn't deserve. Lying in the afterglow of lovemaking, Spencer had admitted that he had just been about to break the silent treatment the night before when Carmen had confronted him in the back yard with her apology.

"If I'd only held on ten more minutes," Carmen teased. "I always lose!" Carmen's heart smiled thinking about their makeup sex.

Those thoughts didn't last long, however, when a sudden and sharp on serge of pain doubled her over. It was all she could do to get her friend to call Spencer and tell him that she was on the way to the doctor. Carmen, of course, knew that something just wasn't quite right. She knew that whatever had just caused this pain wasn't natural and needed to be tended to immediately. Despite protests from her coworkers, Carmen decided to drive the fifteen minutes by herself to meet the doctor who told her to come on in. Spencer was to meet her there as soon as he could.

Spencer was just flying into the doctor's office as the fertility specialist was wrapping up his examination. The nursing attendant ushered him into the consultation area. Rushing in with work boots and muddy jeans, Spencer took a seat beside his obviously pained wife. He took hold of her hand once again. This was becoming a habit. He was constantly consoling her when she cried after starting. It seemed as lately, Carmen was always crying. He could tell by one glance at his wife that she was still obviously in a good deal of pain. Carmen was a strong woman. Spencer knew that if she winced with physical pain then it was real.

The doctor shook Spencer's hand and sat down before he began the conversation. "Carmen, we have probably treated your condition too aggressively. Your body is tired. The clomid has over stimulated your ovaries therefore causing cysts all around your reproductive areas. One of the cysts on your ovaries has ruptured. That is what's causing the sharp pains. This is not necessarily a large threat under normal circumstances."

"But?" Spencer quizzed. He didn't like the look of concern in the doctor's eyes.

"But," the doctor continued. "The problem is compounded because your wife is pregnant."

Spencer and Carmen wanted to leap in the air, but the doctor's disposition kept them grounded momentarily. The doctor continued his explanation.

"I don't want you to get too excited, yet. Your hormone levels are not conducive to a healthy pregnancy and the cysts may or may not contribute to a spontaneous miscarriage.

"How far along am I doctor?" Carmen asked, "and what can I do?"

"Looks like about four weeks, so it's still really early. We need to conservatively treat the cysts while allowing time for the fetus to plant and grow. The truth is that we may have never known about the pregnancy had the cyst not ruptured. Statistics

show that many women conceive but the pregnancy never

takes."

The doctor prescribed bed rest and a mild medicine to shrink the

cysts. Spencer and Carmen decided that although this was the

best news they have had in a while, that it would be best to keep

it their secret until they knew it was safe. At least they now

knew that getting pregnant was not impossible. Both smiled with

trepidation knowing that this would either turn out to be the

answer to all of their prayers or the biggest heartbreak of their

lives. How could they just act normal? The only thing they knew

to do was pray. Carmen almost tiptoed around the house

frightened to take any risks. Four weeks turned into six weeks

and the news was that the cysts had in fact shrunk to some

degree and there was a heartbeat. They heard a heartbeat. A

baby. Although only one heartbeat was heard, the doctor kept

referring to another "spot" that could be another baby hiding

behind the other. Both Spencer and Carmen were ok with that

possibility. In fact, they were ecstatic with that possibility.

"Halfway there" they thought. *"We're half way to the safe period."* Six weeks turned into eight weeks and upon Carmen's visit to the doctor, the news was again the same. The cysts were still there; there was still one heartbeat as well as one spot. She bombarded the doctor with questions. His blanketing answer was to "just wait and see". In Carmen's world, all was good. If they could just reach that golden twelve-week period, then they could forget all of the trouble and move on with their little family to be. All of the Internet health sites and fertility gurus claimed that once twelve weeks pregnant, the mom and baby are safe bar traumatic and unforeseen events. Even Dr. Warren said that twelve weeks was the safe date. At home, they both hinted at baby talk and began making references when alone about their news. The excitement and happiness were inevitable even if they haven't been given the all-clear sign. Carmen, hesitant to get her hopes kept the verbal chatter to a minimum even though she wanted to shout from the rooftops. *"Just a few more weeks,"* she thought. The two weeks before the next checkup proved to be uneventful as well. No more cramps, no blood, yet no morning sickness, all of the

things that the doctor told her to watch for. On one hand Carmen

was on alert for the negative but on the flip side craving to throw

up just to prove the fact that this pregnancy had taken. Soon

enough there would be the "decide all" appointment. Carmen

had circled the date in both blue and pink. The 14th – the date

that the doctor would give the "mom and dad to be" the ok to

share their joy with family and friends. It was very unfortunate

that Carmen would have to make this visit solo. Spencer, bless

his heart, had still been working double shifts to pay off the bill

they had racked. On the bright side, though, they could see the

light at the end of the tunnel as far as that obstacle was

concerned. They both assumed that there would be lots more

doctor visits as well as after birth vacation days that would be

more important, so they were both ok with Carmen going alone.

Although he hated not being there for her, she reassured him

over and over. It was almost all she could do to contain herself

entering the doctor's office. She even had the radiant glow she

had heard so often about. The radiant glow was still present

when she left the doctor's office after her appointment.

WHITE – THE COLOR OF NEW BEGINNINGS

Chapter 6

1995

That whole desperate painstaking journey had led right back to this cold little cubicle she had found herself in. Reality bites. Carmen knew that she couldn't stay in this bathroom stall any longer. Ignoring the inevitable wouldn't change the fact that she couldn't do anything right – not even hold onto the tiny little baby inside her belly. She was once again a failure. Making her legs work now was even harder than when she robotically made her way into this stall some twenty minutes ago. Somehow, she had to muster the courage to walk right back out of this tomb she was in, go tell her loving and excited husband that there hopes had just been flushed down the toilet – literally.

For what it was worth, God had answered one small prayer. Carmen never had to speak a word. She didn't have to admit that she once again was a failure. For when she finally made it back to the table where her husband waited, he knew without words. He had known his wife too long. He had seen this look on Carmen's face before, the disappointment, the anger, the frustration, the sadness, and the emptiness. Somehow, this particular night seemed compounded times ten. It was a look that would never be erased. Spencer instinctively got up, waived the ticket down and escorted his near distraught wife to the car.

As they waited in the hospital emergency room, Carmen was oddly quiet. Spencer kept waiting for the emotional avalanche, but it just didn't happen. In fact, Carmen wouldn't speak at all. She was void of expression, void of words, and void of fight. Spencer was worried. He had never seen her so vulnerable and frail.

About that time, the nurse called the two back into triage. Carmen walked zombie like into the room. The nurse patiently and compassionately asked Carmen questions she just wasn't ready to answer. Carmen just sat there mute and paralyzed with grief, grief for a child never yet born. Spencer apologetically took up a lot of slack filling in details as best as he could. The difficult part, however, was that Spencer knew very little himself. In the restaurant, Carmen mumbled blood – miscarriage – doctor and then they were here. The nurse understood and took them immediately back to the funeral home of pregnancies.

The doctor emerged with sobering and devastating news. Carmen's womb had miscarried the fetus and was in need of a D&C to cauterize and clean the uterine linings of the cysts and leftover carnage from this wreck that had just happened inside Carmen's body. Carmen just rolled over in the clinical bed in a fetal position, a position that she would never witness by an offspring of her own creation. Although Spencer held it together and kissed his mute wife as they rolled her back to surgery, he slid down the waiting room wall completely on all fours and squalled when she was out of sight.

"Dear God, how will I be able to hold it together?" Spencer cried out to a deity that had seemed to abandon him in the last hour. "Why, God, Why?" He just didn't understand why this was happening to them.

An hour later, the doctor informed Spencer that Carmen was through with the procedure and that she would be free to go home the next day. The two dozed away the night, she in a hospital bed and he in the room recliner. Ticks of machines, nurses in and out, and intercoms in the hallway made it very difficult to even try to sleep. Without those factors, sleep would have evaded them. Both dozed interrupted with bad dreams wandering in their subconscious of crying babies and drought-ridden deserts.

After pulling Carmen's Jeep under the portico the next morning, Spencer led Carmen by her elbow and waist as lovingly and comfortably as he knew how. The forty-minute ride home was very sobering. Spencer not knowing how to comfort his wife, what to say, what not to say drove while Carmen stared out the window dazed with either left over anesthesia or the emptiness that had set in over her heart and soul.

"How dare the world go on while my world has stopped?" Carmen thought as they passed pastures and homes and schools. *"What have I done so wrong, God that you are punishing me? Better yet, why are you punishing Spencer? I give up."*

The days after the miscarriage were strange. It was like two people walking around on eggshells not knowing what to say or do. What was there to say or do? Hope had left the little house. Carmen stayed home to recoup for a couple of weeks and did a lot of soul searching so to say. She had read tons of romance novels throughout her life. She never liked when the authors wrote that the characters were going to "find themselves". *"Bologna!"* she would think. She now retracted every negative thought. She knew after this last incident what it meant to search your soul. Better yet, Carmen knew what it meant by searching for the greater good. Carmen had looked into her soul and found nothing but a hole, a hole she couldn't fill.

A few weeks later still searching for answers, Carmen found a corner and cussed God. She cussed herself. Then she apologized to God. She pleaded for God to show her his will and purpose in all of this. Carmen was impatient. God didn't show her anything but an empty house. As much as Carmen discussed and cussed and pleaded and begged with God about baby issues, with Spencer she never discussed it again.

Spencer tiptoed around the subject as well. He didn't want to upset his wife by bringing it up, he didn't want to upset his wife for NOT bringing it up, Hell, he didn't want to upset his wife. These last few years had been agony. He wanted things to just get back to where they used to be. If life happened without a baby, then life happened. He was content with just he and Carmen. They could explore the world. They could travel. They could borrow her students on the weekends, the ones that she claims are pitiful and have nothing. They could spoil them, feel good about it and then send them back. No, he didn't want to adopt, but he wouldn't mind sharing his time and money with less fortunate kids. That would be fun, and they would be free to do as they pleased. Yes, Spencer wanted kids, but he wasn't willing to sacrifice his marriage in the meantime. Sadly, that was exactly what was happening. Carmen walked around the house like a zombie. She was frail and weak from the surgery, from the emotional stress and from the feeling of failure. Spencer was at his wit's end.

One of the qualities Carmen had fell in love with was Spencer's ability to make her laugh. Spencer attempted all of his tricks with no avail. His gestures of humor and wit were received with numb apathy. As well, his attempts for romantic interludes met with the same reaction. Carmen's response was void of the passion and liveliness of her normal self. The relationship they once shared seemed to be dwindling just beyond Spencer's reach. Spencer suggested that Carmen go to the doctor for depression, and that infuriated her. "I can be depressed if I want to, I've just lost a baby!" There was no consolation to be had. Carmen just wanted to hang out in this depth of despair. Spencer even suggested that they start trying again. Carmen nixed that immediately. In fact, she just walked away from that conversation. When Spencer felt as if he didn't know what else to do, he too drifted into a silent behavior. Days after days were spent in minimal and cordial communication and only when warranted. She went back to work. Spencer worked his normal hours plus many overtime hours. They came home, she cooked dinner, he piddled in his shop. They did laundry, they paid bills (including the final bill for all the fertility pills), but that was it. They coexisted, plain and simple. Several months post miscarriage, Carmen checked online to find that the last of her damage to their finances were taken care of. She breathed a sigh of relief and knew it was time. The moment of clarity and restructuring was upon her.

Bright and early the next morning Carmen rose and dressed as if she hadn't in recent months. She actually took the time to apply makeup and pull her hair in that fancy half bun half ponytail that Spencer so often complimented her on. On the long ride to town, Carmen's insides were torn up. She wasn't sure she could do this but had made the agonizing and sacrificing decision that she had come up with a few days after her miscarriage, the day she and God had a pow wow in the corner of her bedroom. She would do it even if it cost her own happiness, her own self-worth and her own emotional demise. Her mind was made up. As her grandmother used to say, it was time to put her big girl panties on.

Walking up to the counter, Carmen prayed for inner strength.

"May I help you?" asked the young and highly attractive receptionist.

"Yes, I have a 10:00 appointment with Mr. Spires."

Sitting in the office waiting, Carmen stared at the nameplate on his desk and all of the college diplomas on the wall.

"Guess my divorce will be just another dollar in his pocket." Carmen muttered out loud. The word, divorce, had actually just spilled out of her mouth. That was only the second time she had ever vocalized the word- once when she called to make the appointment to file for "divorce" and now sitting here, sure she was doing the right thing not for her but for Spencer.

BLACK – THE COLOR OF DESPAIR

Chapter 7

Spencer was beyond mortified when Carmen slid the papers to him across the dining room table that night. Although she had rehearsed the dialogue a thousand times over, she still stumbled and choked up on her words.

"I hope I made the legalities of this easy for you." Carmen stammered out.

"Made it easy for me? How DARE you, Carmen? You're leaving me without as much as a discussion about it? Of all the selfish and misconstrued ideas I've ever heard, this takes the cake. I don't know what to say." Spencer began to spit out words but would lose all thought when he tried to process what Carmen was telling him. "Divorce? Seriously?"

"Just say you forgive me. I'm sure that in time you will accept that this is what I want. I've signed everything that was in both our names back over to you with the exception of my Jeep. I don't expect anything else. The lawyer said because I am not contesting anything that all you have to do is sign and deliver the papers back to him and that will be final."

"Just like that? No! Our marriage, Hell our relationship even before we got married can't just be erased with two damn signatures! Carmen, I understand that you are going through a lot, but it will just take time. You've got to give it time."

"Don't make this harder than it has to be, Spence. I've given it time. I just can't do it anymore. I want a divorce." She lowered her head unable to look into his heart broken eyes.

Carmen knew that the conversation was going to be difficult, but she didn't know that the hole she already had in the pit of her stomach could multiply times ten. Although her mind told her that she was doing the right thing as she readied herself to walk out the door, her heart was tied up in Spencer who was still sitting at the table in disbelief, hands folded and propping up his bowed head. *"He will be alright in time,"* she thought.

Spencer was in complete and utter shock. He was at the point that he didn't know whether to laugh, cry, or shove his fist through the wall. He chose to sit there in silence as Carmen gathered her two suitcases she had already packed and walked towards the door. As she passed Spencer at the table, she slipped an envelope on the table towards his clasped hands. Spencer wouldn't even look at her. As his mind was barraged with all the arguments why he should just grab her and make her stay – he couldn't muster the energy to force his love on her. How had she fallen out of love with him? What had he done? What had he not done? Carmen had to know that he would have fixed anything had she said there was a problem. But that was just it, there had never been any major problems. Sure, there was the baby issue – but that neither of them could do anything about. They had to just give it more time. This, evidently, he couldn't fix. Had she not give him any warning because she just simply didn't love him anymore?

Time had stopped. His world had stopped. A couple of hours later, Spencer only moved when he jumped at the vibration of his phone. Hoping the whole thing had just been a bad dream, he looked down only to see that it wasn't Carmen. He ignored the call.

As he walked to the kitchen window, he wondered where she was going. *"This is ludicrous,"* he thought. Spencer grabbed a glass of water from the sink and took it outside to sit on the back steps. As the sky started turning the orange yellow hue that represented the last hour of daylight, Spencer kept looking for her Jeep lights to emerge from around the curve. He almost made himself believe that the fireflies beginning to come out were actually her headlights. When it was clearly evident that she wasn't coming home way up into the night, Spencer dragged himself into the house and plopped down on the couch not even taking off his work boots.

When he couldn't ignore the alarm chirping any longer, he forced himself to roll off the couch to turn it off, having to dig deep into his pants pockets. Spencer was sore. He didn't know if it was because he slept in his blue jeans, belt, and boots or if it was a sore from being dealt the most devastating heartbreak he had ever known. Realizing she had not texted or called at least to tell him that she had gotten wherever the Hell she was going safely, he started pacing. Emotions pummeled him. Now, he was just plain mad. How dare she just leave? Did he not have a say in this? Should he have recognized some signs that his wife was falling out of love with him? They had never once mentioned separation or divorce ever in their relationship. They both came from families of the Bible Belt – divorce was a taboo not to be discussed. He was sad. Damn, his heart was breaking. He loved Carmen. It crushed his soul that somehow she just stopped reciprocating that love. He had to get to work but somehow her scent just kept him from leaving their little house. He would call her if for no other reason than to make sure she was safe. He was a gentleman after all. He pressed speed dial 1 on his phone. After four rings of a Conway Twitty love song, how apropos at the moment, Spencer heard her pick up only to say, "leave a message after the beep-I'll call you back." Spencer hung up.

Carmen drove pretty much all night. The more distance she put between herself and Spencer would have to make it a little easier, she thought. There would have been no sense in trying to sleep any way. As Carmen fought back tears and exhaustion, she kept telling herself that she was doing the right thing. Being off for the summer would give her time enough to put space between them and allow reality to set in for them both.

Thank God for summer breaks. She really didn't have a plan set in stone. She just knew that her teaching contract had been signed and that she would eventually have to go back. But just like her students, she was off for the summer and would take this time to get things back on track if not for her, for Spence. Most every romance novel she read always had the jilted lover escaping to the Carolinas to some quaint little beach town. Although Carmen didn't have the funds to stay on the water, she thought she would head that way anyhow. She'd figure out something once she got there but planned on renting a hotel room for a short duration. When she had to swerve to avoid oncoming headlights because she was on the wrong side of the yellow line, Carmen went ahead and pulled in a hotel and rented a room. She walked into the double room and realized that she could count on one hand the nights she and Spencer had spent apart. Then, she cried. It was a slobbery, blithering release of despair.

Spencer was late for work for the first time in his entire life. He wasn't his usual self and even the guys noticed it. At lunch he checked his phone. No texts. No missed calls. He tried to call Carmen and again it went straight to her voicemail. He left a message this time that simply said, "This is crazy – come home." He choked up before he could even say bye. He held on to the sound of her speaking if only in her voicemail message. "*What was he going to do?*"

It took everything Carmen had to not answer the incoming call from Spencer. She grasped the phone in her hands when Spencer's photo popped up signaling a call from him. Most days she would just smile when she saw the sweet picture she had snapped without him knowing it. It was the day they walked to the waterfall and he helped her search for rocks for her science lesson. He looked like someone straight out of the fifties with his jeans rolled up wading in the water. Very few men she knew would look as silly just to help his teacher wife find twenty-five examples of sedimentary rocks in the middle of the creek. But today, it just hurt her heart. She held the phone to her cheek knowing that was as close as she would get to him. Will power was hard – but she knew she had to do it. She would work on getting her phone changed soon. That would be second priority right after finding a summer rental.

After driving a couple more hours, Carmen pulled into Hometown Realty in a little town just outside the Folly Beach area. No, it wouldn't be a vacation stay but if she set her mind to it, she would find some things to occupy her mind at least until it wasn't consumed with her marriage and the happily ever after that wasn't going to happen. The day was spent with a local realtor checking out extended stay rentals in the area. Spencer would have found something wrong with every single place she looked at. He would be looking at how much maintenance or repair that would be needed. She betrayed herself by laughing at the thought of what off handed remarks Spencer would make. She couldn't do this. She wasn't at the point where she could recall happy memories. She had to begin letting go or else she risked running back to Spencer's arms. To do that, Carmen rented the most impractical out of the way ramble shack that the realtor offered just because she knew it wouldn't be one that Spencer would allow her to stay in. It was only for the summer after all. Carmen knew in the back of her mind that she would have to at least go back when school started. A thought popped in her mind that maybe she could check out the local schools here. If she liked it, it might benefit her to think about a permanent relocation. Spencer was the only thing that had held her in Georgia as her grandparents had both passed, her parents were divorced and in different areas and her brother and two sisters were distributed all over the state. In fact, Carmen was the only one still living in the original town she grew up in and that was only because she and Spence had fallen in love in high school. She dared not leave up until now. Spencer and her teaching contract that was dated for August 1st were the only two things that bound her to Georgia. Satisfied with the progress for the day, Carmen unlocked the front door and unloaded two small bags of groceries. She settled for a bowl of cereal for supper and sat outside on her temporary home's back steps. How many times had she and Spencer sat on their back steps and just watched the lightning bugs? She was doing it again! No, she wasn't going there. She stood up and took her bowl of cereal to the kitchen bar. Her thoughts still consumed with Spencer, she

fought back the urge to call him. She didn't, and she wouldn't.

Motivated by love, she said a prayer for Spencer's peace and

happiness. Again, she cried herself to sleep.

It was just about all he could do to walk back into their

empty house after work. Even though they had finally paid off

the enormous credit card bill, he was still tempted to continue

working overtime just to avoid walking into this lifeless home.

Nothing mattered in that house without Carmen. She was the

happy in his heart and the smile on his face. She was his

everything. Unfortunately, he wasn't hers. Still questioning how

this crept up on their marriage, Spencer forced himself to

shower for he hadn't in two days. Turning the water up as hot as

he could stand it, Spencer just stood there hoping the scalding

water would just melt his cares away. It didn't work for when

the water finally starting turning tepid, something Carmen

always griped about, he turned it off and stepped out. Not

knowing what to do without their usual nightly routines,

Spencer flipped through the channels not pausing long enough to become interested in anything on tv. When the monotony of sitting on his behind staring at the meaningless shows became too great, Spencer decided to take a walk. He walked down their little country road and when he realized that their neighbor might inquire about his MIA wife, Spencer sped up. He wasn't ready to deal with that just yet. It had been hard enough at work today dodging the guy's questions about why he was so moody and if he had PMS? Normally, Spencer would have ribbed them right back. Today, though, he just grimaced and worked solo as much as possible. Now, it was time to head back home to their king size bed that would seem abnormally big without Carmen beside him. Sleep was sure to evade him and eventually these sleepless nights would catch up with him. But what was he to do? He was at the mercy of his estranged wife who was God knows where. *God, where is she?* Spencer mumbled. *Where is she?*

TRANSLUCENT – THE COLOR OF TEARS

Chapter 8

Carmen didn't realize she would have such a hard time discussing a new phone with the cell carrier rep as she did. She reckoned because it was the last official connection with Spencer and was a little hesitant to break that bond. At the least, she saw his picture pop up on her phone like clockwork every morning before work and every evening, as he was probably getting ready for bed. Most days she got to hear his voice on a voicemail. It was torture to listen to it but would have been more torturous to not. It always tore her insides out. Tonight though, Spencer would probably come unglued when he received the message that "the number you are trying to reach has been disconnected." Carmen walked out of the store with a new phone, a new number, a new contract and a new milestone. Carmen and Spencer had dated all through high school. She had never been all alone, and Spencer was too much of a gentleman to let her handle all of the masculine affairs. Today was a new day. Although her heart still broke, there was the small consolation that she was taking care of herself. She prayed that Spencer would take care of himself. Carmen actually allowed herself to reminisce for a brief moment. She smiled inwardly when it dawned on her that she had done the most sacrificial loving deed that she could imagine. She gave up her love so that Spencer could find new love. And for the first time in a long while, she felt ironically proud.

"The number you are trying to reach is no longer in service" was all that Spencer heard before he crumbled. That small lifeline of hope was gone. The only minute connection he had with the love of his life had just been disconnected. Disconnected is exactly how he felt. He was surviving but not living. Surviving was going to work, coming home from work, showering and possibly grabbing something small to eat. Living was having someone to do all of that for. Carmen had taken that away from him. He couldn't even spill his guts out in the text messages he had been sending regularly. He couldn't tell her that he was sorry any longer, and that he would do whatever it took to get her back. She disconnected him, and they were out of service.

Weeks passed. Spencer functioned and although it wasn't easier, he was getting better at pretending it was. The guys no longer ribbed him about his PMS symptoms. Even though they knew that there had been some type of separation, the crew didn't break the guy code by asking too much. So, for the most part, Spencer got to keep a minimum of discretion when it came to his failure as a husband. The outward appearance and behavior improved but he still needed to somehow repair the giant gash right down the middle of his heart.

A month and a half after the day his world crashed, Spencer even stopped at the grocery store and ran in to pick up a few things. He always laughed when Carmen said that because she inevitably came in with ten bags past a few things. He chuckled because he now knew the struggle. With some consolation Spencer realized that he had just laughed at a Carmen memory rather than cry. He supposed that was a positive sign. There wasn't a doubt in his mind that he would never get over Carmen but after the last several weeks at least his body showed signs of recovery. Physical recovery might be easy, but the emotional recovery would never come Spencer

feared. Carmen cutting off all ties with the phone deal just signed

sealed and delivered the fact that she wanted to move on and

was serious about forgetting about him and what all they had. He

reckoned it was time to consider his life without her in it.

Carmen wandered the cobblestone road of Main Street in

the little town ten minutes from her summer home. She had

visited each little antique shop and even bought a piece or two.

Her favorite one named "Rust & Ruffles" was run by a little old

lady and her husband. The sweet elderly woman wanted to tell

her the story of every single piece in their collection. Each had a

history and a story behind it. Because Carmen was never in a

hurry to get anywhere, she always listened. Sometimes her

husband would come out from the back and his wife would call

him "Old Crotchedy". Although the words were demeaning, the

little old lady said it with a hint of sassiness and a whole lot of

love. It was easy to feel the warmth between them and easier to

see it when Norman, the crotchedy husband, placed his arm

around his wife in a way that still evoked possessiveness and unfathomable adoration. After a few visits, Carmen learned that

they had been married for over sixty years. The little old lady

named Irene and Carmen became fast friends. Irene was good at

suggesting advice that Carmen never asked for but would say it

in such a way that Carmen never took offense. It was as if she

and her grandmother were having a casual conversation.

Carmen thought of Spencer and their past discussions of

growing old together. That had always been the plan. That one

day they would be old and gray watching their grandkids play in

the yard. Reminiscing about their relationship broke her heart

again. Carmen had to stop doing that. Now, Spencer would be

able to find someone new, grow old with her, and have her call

him "Old Crotchedy". On the days she drove to town, Carmen

always visited Ms. Irene. Then she usually ended up in the center

park overlooking the wharf. She always took a bag of sunflower

seeds to throw to the birds and squirrels. She would sit there for

a good part of the afternoon observing. She was getting pretty

good at distinguishing the locals from the tourists. She actually

liked it here. The romance novels were right. Coastal town

charm draws you in and won't let you leave. Had it not been for her teaching contract, Carmen could make this her home. Home, she thought was a word meant for a family. She was only a family of one, so she thought probably residence would be a better term for where she lived. Maybe she should think about getting a dog. She was of no use to anyone but her students and possibly a pet. Yes, that would be on her agenda. Carmen was getting good at agendas. She managed to survive by making small term goals. Long-term plans were not working for her, so she took one day at a time. Oh, how her body and heart longed to tell Spencer about the antique tea set she purchased from Irene and the story of how Norman got it for her after trading it for work on the town mayor's house because his wife wanted some fancy woodwork in their parlor. Norman wouldn't take money but asked for the tea set for his new bride because he thought he would never be able to afford such a set. Now that they were in their mid 80s, they were actually selling off some of their pieces to supplement their retirement income. That was the kind of husband Spencer was, Carmen thought. He was a lot like

Norman. He was always sacrificing his money and wants to put Carmen first. A prime example was the fact that he had taken it upon himself to work all of those long overtime hours just to pay off Carmen's debt. She thought to herself what a wonderful man he was and what a perfect husband he had been to her and will be again. This made Carmen actually feel better because she was finally reciprocating that kind of love. In a warped way, she realized that she was sacrificing her happiness and desires to assure that Spencer would eventually get his. When the streetlights popped on due to the setting sun, Carmen walked back to her Jeep feeling good about her decision for the first time in weeks. She even turned on the radio and flipped through stations until she found some upbeat song to sing along with.

Spencer looked at the calendar and realized that he had not spoken to Carmen in over seven weeks, seven long agonizing weeks. With the exception of a lot of dust on the furniture and cups and saucers left unwashed, the house still carried her sweet scent. Oh, how he wanted to talk to her. His mind continually thought of her. His heart ached for her. He longed to wrap his arms around her. He still just couldn't believe this was real. The inevitable truth of this situation was going to have to sink in. He forcibly tried to digest that their marriage was over. It was at that very moment, an idea bombarded his thoughts. He decided to do what any single man would do. He would go to the bar and get drunk. Why had he not thought of that earlier? If it only helped him forget the misery he was wallowing in for a brief time, then it would be worth it. Deciding to go to a bar fifty miles down the road was probably a good idea because small town rumors had only just begun to surface about why the Simpkins were separated. He just wasn't ready to deal with it. Alcohol might in fact just make him punch someone if they said anything. Adding to that sense of being responsible, he even called one of his buddies to go with him as the designated driver. Yep, Carmen wouldn't be on his mind at all after about three Tall Boys. "*Best decision in a while,*" he thought.

Plans were going perfectly three hours later. Killing his second big boy, Spencer and Lance finished up a game of pool. Carmen's name had not entered his mind, and he was genuinely enjoying a guy's night out. Lance decided to work the dance floor to "try to get some action" while Spencer climbed up on one of the bar stools, ordered another big boy, grabbed a bowl of peanuts and focused on the game playing on the big screen behind the mirrored bar.

"Your friend sure has some moves"

Spencer realized someone was talking to him. When he turned to see, he realized that someone was wearing tight blue jeans and a halter-top that pushed her prizes up on two pedestals. Trying not to stare, Spencer turned the opposite way to see Lance cutting a move between two similar looking girls on the dance floor both wearing cowboy hats, blue jean shorts and one-sided halter tops. Spencer giggled. Lance looked like a peacock out strutting his stuff in a long lost mating ritual. When the guys' eyes met, Lance winked at his buddy, confirming his good time.

Without looking at the girl on the stool beside him, he replied. "Yes, he does." Spencer didn't elaborate. This was an awkward situation. Spencer may have been married for a long time, but he knew how casual bar encounters worked. He had only wanted to come get drunk and even after two beers, he felt only a small buzz. Not once had he thought about the stereotypical bar hoppers he might encounter. He should have thought ahead. Even so, Spencer was never one to be rude.

"I know this sounds like a come on, but I've never seen you in here before," she said. "I'm Julie."

"Only because I've never been here before. I'm Spencer." Spencer offered still trying not to be rude but trying not to be encouraging either. In his mind there was a great debate going on. Julie was cute. Not his type but cute. Hell, why shouldn't he have a friendly flirty conversation with a cute girl? What was wrong with that? His wife had filed for divorce. He was practically the same as Lance out there. The difference was Lance was begging for sex, Spencer was trying to watch a ballgame. He sat still not committing one way or the other.

Julie pursued, "Well I'm glad you're here. Not much to look at in here lately. You are a breath of fresh air. What's your story, Spencer?"

"Not much of a story. I'm just here for the beer."

"Oh, you're the mysterious type, huh?" Julie teased. "I like that."

Spencer had been right. She was definitely flirting and by his gut instinct he would be able to take it as far as he wanted. He knew the bar type girls. His crew discussed them every single Monday after an alcohol filled weekend at the honky tonks. Although Spencer had never desired such activity, he thought just for a minute that maybe a one night roll in the hay wild sex might just help him get over this hump he was in. The anger he felt to be in this situation won out, and he turned and smiled at Julie.

"So, what's your story, Julie?" he quizzed while signaling the bartender to refill her drink.

"Same story different day. Here with my girlfriends" pointing at the same group of girls still two stepping with Lance. "Just have higher standards" she laughed. "You have a different vibe going on."

"Oh, I do, do I?" Lance actually liked this feeling of being flirted with. Carmen didn't want him. *NO!* he thought. *I will not think of Carmen. She's gone.*

"Want to dance? There's a slow song coming on."

After only a brief hesitation, Spencer answered. "Sure, why not?"

Boy, had it been a long time since Spencer held another woman in his arms. As he and Julie slow danced, he felt her nestle in a little closer. A red flag of morality popped in his head and just as quickly he waved it away. He was feeling good, almost carefree. The third beer had kicked in and the tingling in his groin gave way to the ethical argument in his head. They danced. Luckily two more slow songs played immediately in a row. Spencer pulled Julie closer and smelled her hair. The scent of sweet pea rose only added to the sexual tension he was beginning to feel. Swaying back and forth to the tune, Spencer held Julie by the small of her back while she looked up at him. As the music came to an end, she reached up on tiptoes and gently kissed him on his bottom lip seductively biting it as an invitation for more. Spencer didn't protest. As she grabbed him by the hand and pulled him back to the bar, he saw Lance give him a thumbs up as they walked past. At the bar Julie smiled. She asked did he want another beer because she thought she would have one more shot. Spencer waved down the bartender and in fact ordered another for himself. As they talked in generalities, Spencer felt Julie's legs and knees begin to knead and intertwine between his. Then she actually placed her hand on his thigh and giggled about something he said. His stomach knotted up. His loins began to heat up and throb. After her latest shot of tequila, she stood up and wiggled her way between his legs on the barstool and wrapped her arms around his neck to whisper in his ear.

Here was Spencer's chance. The suggestion Julie whispered in his ear was all the invitation he needed to leave now and take his sexual frustration out on her. He could release all of this pinned up anger and tension he had. In her own words, Spencer could do whatever he wanted to with her. The thought of driving himself into a very endowed woman over and over throughout the night excited him. He missed the taste of hot sweat under a woman's thigh. He loved taking it slow and building until she would beg for release. Sex would be good. A one-night stand might even help detach his emotional state as of late. No strings attached, he thought. Was there a line drawn? Was Spencer about to cross it?

Julie noticed Spencer's delayed response but could see the want in his eyes. She knew he was at the edge, and she couldn't wait to show him how real cowgirls rode. "So, what will it be?" "Now or after a few more beers?"

"You just don't strike me as the one-night stand kind of girl" Spencer teased. "Who said it would be a one night stand, cowboy?" "I think you'll like what you get so much you might come back for more." Julie teased right back. She had never been one to have to beg for companionship. Somehow this guy proved a challenge. She liked challenges.

"Oh, I already like what I'm getting." Spencer's heart tremored. It had definitely been a while since he had been this aroused. He longed for uninhibited, raw passion reminiscent of his younger days.

"Besides it's not like you're married or anything" Julie teased as she nibbled his ear.

"Not like you're married," Spencer thought. *"What the hell was he doing? He was married."* In fact, the large envelope Carmen had slid to him across the table now almost two months ago had never been opened nor signed. Opening it and signing the papers would signal an official ending. He hadn't been ready for that. Neither was he ready for what was going on right between his legs. He had never cheated on Carmen and although for all sense and purposes they were half way divorced, he wouldn't start now. Technicalities. Some easy lay was not worth the regret he would have in the morning. It wasn't fair to anyone because he knew that if he lay on top of this girl who so freely offered, he would be seeing Carmen.

Spencer bolted up and threw some cash on the bar. "I'm sorry, Julie. You're a beautiful girl. You should look for more meaningful relationships than with men like me in a bar like this." Spencer waved Lance down and headed out of the honky

tonk. He kicked his truck tire before climbing in.

"Dang, Spencer I had just about talked BOTH them girls

into something!" Lance protested.

"Take me home!" Spencer demanded.

ORANGE – THE COLOR OF LUST

Chapter 9

Carmen looked at the calendar. August was quickly approaching. In fact, she had even received the customary end of summer email this morning about times to report for teacher workdays. The inevitable was going to happen. Her lease ran out in two weeks. Thinking about getting back to reality, Carmen also realized that she hadn't received any emails or calls from her lawyer. Surely, everything was final by now. That was something else to put on her agenda. The next couple of weeks would be busy. Also, on her agenda was contacting her co-teacher. She had offered to let Carmen rent out her fully furnished basement while Carmen looked for something more permanent. She was seriously considering fulfilling this year's contract in Georgia while hunting a teaching job in Carolina. Her heart tugged when she thought of leaving Irene and Norman. They had both become almost surrogate grandparents in the short time she had known them. Despite the constant barrage of memories that evaded Carmen's heart and soul, she actually liked it here. The romance novels proved true. The Carolinas were peaceful, but for now she had to prepare for the trip back

to Georgia. Carmen was a stickler for details. She had everything

lined up and ready. What she wasn't ready for was the

possibility of running into Spencer. That was highly likely in such

a small town. As her mind wandered from what he was doing to

how he was doing, she forced herself to block those thoughts.

Thoughts like that only haunted Carmen and pushed memories

from her eyes in form of tears.

Spencer was still cursing himself for what had happened

when he stumbled in the house well after midnight. Sleep would

evade him, once again, he knew so he went to brew a cup of

coffee. Maybe that would ward off the hangover that was sure to

pursue. *"How did he let what happened happen?"* He felt guilty

and ashamed. As he sat at the round dining table to wait on his

coffee to perk, he realized that he hadn't sat there since the day

Carmen left. Sitting in the same position, as he was when she

crushed his life, he spotted the large orange envelope she slid

over to him that day. It sat in the same spot unopened. In it was a

divorce waiting for a signature. "Easy" she had said. *"She thinks* ending our relationship will be easy," he thought. She had lost her

mind. Should he open it? Should he at least peruse the details of

their marriage demise? If he had already signed it would he feel

so guilty about what happened tonight? Would not signing it

make this nightmare go away? If he ignored it would Carmen

come home? As the coffee pot whistled, Spencer pushed away

from the table and poured him a cup of coffee in the mug that

Carmen bought for him from the souvenir shop at Yellowstone

last spring. "Wanting her is not going to make her come home."

Halfway through the second cup of coffee and three Tylenols,

Spencer made the decision to open the envelope if nothing else

but to see Carmen's signature. If she wanted the divorce, then

she would get it. He would sign the documents. He braced

himself and slipped the contents out on the table. The first

several pages were legal mumbo jumbo, phrases Spencer barely

could pronounce much less understand. Looked like standard

lawyer jargon. Carmen had made sure that everything was

outlined in detail. She had always been that way. She was the

most organized person he knew sometimes to a fault. She always had an itinerary and deviated very little from it. Sometimes that was a good thing. She would get so much accomplished by her planning. Other times Spencer would pick at her and tell her to take time to smell the roses or go with the flow. They would both laugh because they balanced each other so well. Spencer continued to peruse the document. It was just as she had said. All properties had reverted back to his name only with the exception of the Jeep. One day he would probably appreciate the fact that she hadn't taken everything except the kitchen sink. Many of his divorced friends talked about their exes leaving them high and dry. Almost all of their friends had been divorced. Spencer anguished at the fact that they too would join their ranks. The next to the last page was the signature page. He gasped when he saw Carmen's signature. Scrolled curly lines ending her love for him. *Carmen L. Simpkins.* All it would take was his signature to be final. Spencer still avoided signing it persuading himself that he didn't have a pen and would sign it in the morning. The last page was smaller than the other documents. Turns out Spencer's heart skipped a beat when he saw regular notebook paper with Carmen's beautiful handwriting. Why hadn't she told him she had left a letter? He thought it had only been the lawyer's documents. Why had it taken him all summer long to open it? Dang it, she may have told him where it was that she was going. Oh, he was stupid. Spencer went to the couch to settle in to read Carmen's letter. He took a deep breath and braced himself for the explanation as to what he had done so wrong that Carmen stopped loving him.

Dear Spence,

As you read this I'm sure you are in shock. I know you never expected what I threw at you today and for that I am so sorry. Had I talked to you about it, I wouldn't have been strong enough to go through with it. Trust me when I say I know this is the best decision for you. I pray that you will keep an open mind and know that I did not make this decision lightly. I know you will go through a period of anger at me, and I don't blame you. I deserve your anger for I have put you through way more than what is fair. You, my Spence, deserve far more than I have given you. All that I have left is the only thing that I can give you worth giving. I am giving you a new chance. You are the best man I have ever had the honor of knowing. Please be mad at me only for a short time. Please know that I am divorcing you out of love. Thank you for loving me for as long as you have and as completely as you have. Maybe in time you can reflect on our memories with fondness and possibly even share them with your grandchildren. Don't grieve for what we have lost. Remember what we had but pursue love again. That is my wish for you.

Always,

Carmen

Spencer read and reread the letter numerous times. How dare she make such a decision and then claim it to be for him? Although he was completely devastated, he finally understood the rationale behind her choice. All along he had thought she just stopped loving him or worse that maybe she had found someone else. He was so wrong. She loved him more than she had loved herself. She was taking herself out of the picture so that he could find someone else that could give him children. Why hadn't she

talked to him about it? He would have begged and begged her to

stay arguing that her love was worth more than anything in this

world and that he only wanted her. He didn't need to have

children. He only wanted her. But he now knew she knew that

would have been his argument. She would have expected him to

give up a family in order to continue life with her. She had made

this stupid, self-sacrificing, honorable, crazy decision out of love

for him. Although he loved her more than he ever thought

possible at this very moment, he cussed her foolishness.

GRAY – THE COLOR OF ANGUISH

Chapter 10

Carmen packed her Jeep with the last few of her belongings. It didn't take but a couple of boxes to carry what she had left of this life, as she knew it. In the weeks before her divorce disclosure, Carmen secretly packed her most sentimental items in a box and the remainder of her clothes and stored them in a rented storage unit down town. Carmen was proud of the fact that although emotionally devastated, she thought ahead enough to avoid having to confront Spencer after the fact. Twelve weeks had in once sense flown by. She wasn't ready to be flung back into reality. Heading back to school would be fine. She missed the children. But every corner she turned would have some memory of her Spence. Even at work, there were remnants of him. When she first got her job, he made bookshelves and cubbies for her classroom. He often came up to the school after hours to help. That was just in her little class. The town was so small, and they had such a history in it, it would be impossible to ignore all the little memories of them there. On the other hand, the last twelve weeks were the longest of her life.

Every day had been emotionally draining and long void of company. Had it not been for the company of her newfound friends, Irene and Norman, Carmen may not have survived. In another sense, Carmen felt like she had spent a lifetime with Irene and Norman. They were already implanted in her heart, and she almost couldn't bear to leave them. Her soul was refreshed to a certain extent. She was at peace with her decision and hoped that Spencer was beginning to look for new happiness. As she looked around the little cottage she was leaving, she refrained from calling it home. Home was where the heart was. Although her heart was in Georgia with Spencer, she settled for the fact that she had successfully went through with her plan and gave Spencer time to accept her decision. Carmen smiled. She pulled down the gravel road that led her away from the journey that helped search her soul. She had planned on making just two stops. One was to gas up for the long drive. The second would prove the hardest. She had to stop by Irene and Norman's and try to find the words of goodbye. In this short time, she had been here, Carmen had come to love Irene no less than she did her own grandmother. Although Norman honored Irene and Carmen's daily tea times with his absence, her heart tugged at the thought of him in his white shirt, khaki slacks, and spirited bowties that changed colors daily. Norman was a saint. The couple often wanted Carmen to "sit a spell" or "stay for supper" and there was of course the daily tea and cake in Irene's parlor. Irene instinctively knew the troubles Carmen was fighting and prodded and nudged enough that eventually the complete story came out. Irene was not judgmental and listened and consoled and offered a tissue when needed. Carmen's heart was not cured over tea and crumpets but often Irene's dainty little wrinkled hand would hold Carmen's until the jab in her heart was dull rather than sharp.

Irene had asked Carmen to stop by before she left. Even though that wasn't a question that needed to be asked, Carmen sweetly promised. The little bell above the door dinged when Carmen entered. Irene wiped her hands on her blue gingham apron and wistfully smiled at Norman.

"She needs this, you know," Norman whispered.

"I know, old man," Irene smiled and kissed the top of his silver hair.

"You're still beautiful," Norman replied.

"And you're still crotchedy with bad eyes," she said.

Irene came out from behind the curtain that separated their living quarters from their shop to give Carmen a giant hug.

"There's my girl!" Irene squealed and held on just a little tighter and longer than normal. "Can you come sit a spell and have some tea one more time with an old woman?"

Carmen really needed to be on the road and had only come by for a quick hug goodbye but just couldn't tell her elderly friend no. To be truthful, Carmen didn't know if she could endure another heart wrenching goodbye.

As they entered Irene's tearoom, Carmen marveled that one of Irene's finest tea sets was already in place and complimented by fresh banana bread lovingly placed on the matching tiered plate.

"You're going to make me fat, Ms. Irene!" Carmen whined.

"Not today. Today, I'm going to make you understand." Irene stated plainly.

As they sat, Irene handed her a weathered and tattered photo album.

"Go ahead, flip through my life," Irene prodded.

Carmen took the book tenderly, fearful that the pages would disintegrate.

"Is this you, Irene?"

"That was me right after Norman proposed on one of his few weekend furlos."

"You are so beautiful."

"After the third proposal, I figured I better say yes."

They laughed. Irene really was a witty person. Carmen bet she was a feisty young lady as well.

Carmen continued to flip through the pages and commented on various photos that caught her eye. As well, Irene paused to explain pictures from special occasions and places the couple had been.

"Here we are while building our first house" and "here's Norman and his handsome self right after he was discharged from the Army. I remember that day as if it were this morning. I just couldn't wait to get my hands on him when he got off that train." Irene giggled. "So, I pulled him down the back lane between the general store and Old Mae Hinson's dress shop and gave him some loving right then and there."

"Ms. Irene, you're gonna make me blush."

The old lady fanned the air. "Well he'd been gone for over six months and penning letters to him just never worked up a sweat." Irene chuckled.

Carmen paused and smiled. "You love him as much now as you did then?"

"No, I love him more even if he is crotchedy but hold that thought, Dear."

They continued their journey down memory lane.

"Look here, Carmen. Here is when we took our first vacation. Norman and me drove all the way to Niagara Falls in Canada. And this is a clipping from the newspaper when me and

Norman won the blue ribbon for our prize jams at the County Fair." Irene seemed to be lost in thought. Carmen patiently waited as her friend stared at moments in time. She waited until Irene turned the page.

A few more pictures that the feisty little lady narrated were the picture of Norman when he was ordained as deacon of the Shady Grove church, the photo of a car that Norm had restored from scratch, a picture of a fishing trip complete with Irene in waders and Norman carrying rods and bait. As such, Irene summarized each and every photo they viewed.

Carmen flipped several pages that had no pictures on them. "Oh, that's too bad. What happened to these photos Ms. Irene?"

"Keep flipping, Carmen." Irene nudged.

Carmen obeyed. Towards the end of the book, the photos resumed. It was obvious that Irene and Norman had both aged but were again chronologically time lined using photos of their exploits, happenings and milestones. When the last photo had been discussed at length, Carmen simply closed the book and ran her hand across the leather basking in the glorious life of her newfound friend.

"Thank you for sharing."

Irene grasped Carmen's hands in both of hers. "What did you notice, Carmen?"

"I'm not sure what you are asking. I noticed a lot of photos of you and Norman and important times in your life." Irene flipped back to the last page right before the blank ones. There was a picture of Irene and Norman together. Irene had a flowing dress, Buxton shoes and a hat with a single flower on the rim.

"That was a pink wildflower Norm picked for me just for the occasion. Of course, you can't tell that because our photos were still black and white back in the old days."

Norm had on a nice suit for the era, and he too wore a hat. What stood out most was the absence of a smile on either of them unlike the rest of the album. Carmen hadn't noticed on the first go round.

"There's sadness in this picture."

Irene nodded in agreement. "As custom in those days, you can't tell my situation because of my flowing gown, but I had just given birth two weeks before this picture was taken."

"Oh, Irene. I've never heard you talk of your children."

"Carmen, look closer."

Carmen held the album closer to her vision level and noticed a tiny hand carved cross in the background just behind the solemn couple. She winced.

"Irene, noooo. Is that what I think?"

Irene restrained the tears for she knew she needed to get through this conversation. Still sixty-five years later, the tears lurked just behind her lids. They were ready to flow at any given moment.

Carmen waited. She knew her friend would continue when she was ready. It was Carmen's time to place her hand on her friend's as had been reciprocated so many times this summer.

"Oh, I was the second happiest person in the world at that time. Norman of course was the happiest. He spoiled me rotten.

Wouldn't let me lift a finger. Did all of the housework and laundry and made me apple fritters each week. He crafted a cradle in his spare time from scrap wood he brought home from work. We were going to be good parents. Irene paused. Back then, however, medicine wasn't like it is today. Our angel, little Darcy, had a time coming into this world, a fighter she was. The circuit doctor wouldn't be back into town until the next day, so when my pains started, Norman went for my mother and his sister right away. It was our first child and we had no clue what was going on. I think Norm ran all the way to their house in his long johns" Irene snickered.

"Anyway, labor lasted all night and pretty much into the next day. Back then, men weren't allowed in the birthing room. But my screams frightened him and although my mom ran him out two or three times, the fourth time he planted himself at my head and wiped my brows. He said he would never leave my side. He was right there the whole time. He said I started fading, but all I remember about that day was fighting unconsciousness and the dizziness and the pain. I concentrated on pushing and willing my little Darcy to come on out. The doctor finally arrived a little after I fell into some gray haze between reality and oblivion. The rest is still fuzzy, but Norman filled me in on how the doctor struggled to pull Darcy from my pelvis. Her shoulders were wide and as he twisted and maneuvered her little pink self, my body contorted with pain. Norman experienced the pain right along with me. His sister later told me that he wiped my brow, held my hand and repeatedly coaxed me throughout my labor. But the next thing I remember is the biggest gush of physical relief and the most beautiful cry I had ever heard in my life." Again, Irene paused. .

"Irene, Irene wake up, Darcy is here. Our daughter is here." Norman cried.

"I willed my heart to beat. I willed my lungs to contract. I willed my uterus to cauterize itself from somewhere deep inside my soul. And it did."

"The sound of my daughter made me rebound quickly, and I reached for my angel to suckle. Although Darcy had just fought for two days to enter this world, she didn't look none the ware. She was the most beautiful thing I had ever seen. All parents say that but what I tell you is the truth. She was pink and round and had just a speck of strawberry blonde hair around her petite ears. Her lips were shaped just like Norman's and my heart was full." Irene closed her eyes as if she was visualizing the image of her little child in her mind. "Darcy latched on to my breast and tried to nurse. I didn't notice at first but evidently the Doc and my mom did. My milk was coming but only pooling in Darcy's mouth. It wouldn't go down."

Carmen wiped a tear from her eyes. She could see the anguish in her friend's eyes even after all this time. Again, Irene hesitated in order to regain strength enough to finish her story. She had to finish the story.

"The labor was very strenuous on Darcy. Doc had pulled and pulled just trying to manipulate her shoulders free from my womb. In the process, Darcy's little neck was broken. There was no such thing as caesareans back then. Darcy lived two weeks. For two weeks of my life, I was a mommy. "

Tears flowed heavily by both women. They didn't even pretend they weren't there. They let them run freely.

After a few moments of silence and recuperation, Irene continued with tissue in hand.

"This, Carmen, was when I thought my life ended. I stopped living about this time. Norman stopped living about this time."

"Why did I tell you this story, Carmen?"

"I'm not sure, Irene. But it means so much to me for you to share this most personal memory."

"Carmen, flip through the album again starting at the picture we just discussed."

Carmen obliged. The picture of the couple in front of Darcy's grave preceded several blank pages. Eventually new photos dated several years later of Norman and Irene reemerged.

"The blank spaces are all the missed opportunities and missed memories with Norman. I stopped living. I stopped loving. I stopped functioning. I was an empty shell of a woman. I was a body void of a soul. I was a wife void of purpose. Norman, God bless his soul, stood beside me as our lives fell apart. Day by day, he forced me to eat, forced me to live and forced me to love him. He was the most stubborn man. There were more times than I can count that I cussed him and attempted to throw him out of my life. That, my dear, was when he earned the nickname, "Old Crotchedy". He just wouldn't have any of it. He badgered me and badgered me. To hear him tell it, he forced enough love in our marriage during that time for the both of us. And it's true. He breathed for me. I didn't realize it but slowly I started working with him and not against him. Now I know you don't have much time, girl, just realize initially, I bucked defiantly. I only functioned to appease him. My progress was not sure and fast enough for Norman. But then one day, he brought me wildflowers."

As if on cue, Norman walked in behind Irene and placed his hand on her shoulder.

"You tell her the rest, sweetie." Irene suggested.

95

With a reminiscent look, Norman began. "I saw these wildflowers at the end of our land just beneath the old Live Oak tree. They were pink and were like none I had ever seen in our area before. Almost reluctant to steal the beauty they brought to the little hillside, I only took a few. I thought maybe they would bring a smile to my despondent wife. Between the walk back from the wildflower area to our little home, I named the flowers "Pink Darcies", and I decided that day was the day things had to change, come what may."

Norman looked to Irene for permission.

"It's ok hon, go on."

Norman continued, "I can't explain it, but I wasn't mad at God. Sure, he had taken Darcy from us, but he had also given her to us. Right or wrong, I was mad at Irene. For some reason at that particular moment anger just consumed my heart. I was furious. I was angry that Irene had given up. She had been robbing us of time. I stormed into our bedroom because I knew that was where she would be. She had been there since we placed Darcy in the ground. She was despondent and depressed.

But something just came over me. I thrust the flowers to Irene, told her to get dressed that Darcy deserved some flowers and I meant right then."

Irene interrupted. "That was the first and only time Norm demanded that I do something with such urgency and animosity. So, I did."

Norman continued, "We went to the grave and we cried tears of grief and tears of blessings. God had blessed us with Darcy if only for just a short time. For two weeks, our life was blessed with this little angel. Removing ourselves from life would be dishonoring her memory. I told Irene. We must live for Darcy."

"And so, we did," Irene said looking up and smiling at her husband. "It wasn't easy, but we took it day by day. Life eventually crept back into my body and Norm and I resumed living. Things were good, but she concluded her story by adding, "Darcy's neck wasn't the only thing damaged in the labor. My insides were destroyed, and I never got pregnant again."

Carmen wiped the mascara running from her eyes. "I'm so sorry, Irene. I'm so sorry, Norman. That had to be devastating."

Irene patted Carmen's hand. "Dear, there's a reason we're telling you this. There's not one picture in this photo album of our life that you see us with child. Bar one photo, every single snapshot into our 60 plus years of marriage is a glimpse of a happy memory. The empty spots are wasted time, wasted memories, and wasted happiness." Irene paused. She wiped a tear from Carmen's eye and gently lifted her face to make eye contact. "Honey, my life has been complete. Yours can too. I've lived my happily ever after, and now it's your turn. Quit wasting moments."

Understanding seeped into Carmen's mind. She sat back to contemplate this tragic story and how it applied to her life. *How does she do that?* Carmen wondered. Irene had known just how to mend Carmen's heart.

Norman and Irene on the façade of cleaning up, gathered plates and cups and headed to the kitchen.

Carmen wiped her eyes one last time and found her way to the couple standing at the kitchen sink washing dishes together. Their back was to her. She paused only to thank God for this sweet, precious little couple that he had put in her path. This journey she had been on ironically had just changed. She grabbed them together, hugged them as tightly as she could and mumbled, "Thank You! I love you both big!" She all but ran out the door.

Although several hours later than anticipated, Carmen was on the road headed south.

BROWN – THE COLOR OF REVELATION

Chapter 11

Spencer knew that he couldn't call Carmen, but an idea miraculously popped into his head. He jumped up to look at the calendar. He checked online to see when the first day of school was. Emotional tragedy causes you to do stupid things as well as not do common sense things that would ordinarily be routine. Why hadn't he thought about it? Carmen had to report to work later this week. He remembered her signing her contract at the end of the year, and she was not the type of person that wouldn't fulfill her obligations. With a renewed hope, Spencer knew he had to address what had been nagging him for the last twelve weeks. She would listen to him. It had been his fault after all, and he finally knew how to fix it if it wasn't too late.

Carmen had made a mistake but not on purpose. The decision she thought was right at the time only changed after hearing Irene and Norman's story. Should she call? Should she text? Should she just show up back at the house? Would he forgive her? Had she already found someone else? Questions and concerns popped in her head like kernels of corn. Confused and conflicted, Carmen had to make a plan. She pulled off the interstate to refuel. She was halfway home and still hadn't figured out exactly how to correct this mess she had made. Although she was highly anxious to get there, Carmen sat in the Jeep to make up her mind. She knew it was a cop out to send a text but didn't need to get into an emotional conversation over the phone. She wanted to explain everything to him face to face.

Spencer's phone vibrated. Although he had long given up on contact from his estranged wife, he checked it anyway but didn't recognize the number that was texting him.

"I don't expect you to understand but if it is not too late, meet me where we first met – tonight at 9:00"

His heart dropped. Was it truly her? His mind raced a million ways past Sunday. What was this all about? Why after all of this time? Considering all options both good and bad, Spencer's conclusion was that she had probably forgotten something at their house, correction "his house" something she had made sure to clarify. But why had she sent such a cryptic message? Should he go or should he make her suffer as he had for the last three months? He knew the answer even before he asked himself such questions. There was no thinking about it. Even if it turned out to be in fact a meeting to discuss legalities on neutral terms, Spencer would at least get to see the person he missed most in this world. Of course he'd be there, and he knew without a doubt the meeting place she referred to.

Carmen was already driving well past the speed limit, but she hadn't accounted for the time she needed to stop and grab something out of her storage unit. Her worst nightmare would be that he wouldn't show up. Her second worst nightmare would be that he would show up, she'd be late, and he'd leave. Then there was the possibility that he'd show up but not forgive her. Carmen accelerated even more. Her heart raced as fast as the speedometer showed.

Spencer made sure the crew didn't lag today. He needed time to do a few things after work and shower. "Should he run by and get a haircut? Come to think of it, he hadn't had one since before Carmen left. He thought he would. He flogged the crew even more because he had just added that to his "to do" list.

Should he get flowers? Toiling with that decision, he told himself he would wait and weigh the pros and cons before heading to their spot. Although he longed to see her, he did have a little pride. He didn't want it to appear as begging Deep down, though, he knew if it came to that then he would beg. After a quick stop at the barber shop, Spencer went home to shower and mentally prepare for seeing Carmen. The hot steam released some of his anxiety and loosened up the knot that had formed between both shoulders. Picking out what shirt to wear had never been a problem until now. You'd thought it was Spencer's first date as nervous as he was. Spotting the picture on the nightstand of the two on their first cruise, he spoke to her as he had for weeks on end. "So, what's it gonna be, my love? I'll be there shortly."

Spencer thought best to tidy up some just in case she came home with him. Dressed and ready, Spencer headed to the door before realizing he had neglected to do what was needed most. He walked straight back to the bedroom and knelt beside his bed. It had been far too long since he had a good conversation with God.

"Dear Lord, I'm sorry about my behavior recently, and I'm sorry I've not talked to you about it. I wish I could change things, but you know my heart. God, will you please give me the strength to do what I need to do tonight?"

Carmen pilfered through the plastic tubs stored in her unit. After only two unsuccessful tries, she found what she needed. With excitement building, Carmen had just enough time to make it to the spot where the rest of her life would be decided. Dusk had fallen but the late summer night was still smothering. The "dog days of summer" in Georgia were unpredictable. The heat of the day generally brought afternoon thunderstorms, and tonight looked no different. As the thunder rolled and the dark sky darkened a few minutes before 9:00, Carmen pulled in and parked at she and Spencer's alma mater's softball field. She had not seen Spence's truck. She couldn't have missed it had it been there. These fields had been abandoned years ago due to the new by pass through town. This place where Carmen and Spence first met, nestled at the back of hundreds of acres of farmland seemed interrupted only by the moonlight and the sounds of whippoorwills. That was now. Of course, throughout high school this was the happening place. Practice every day and a long season, Carmen spent many tiring hours right here. She loved it. Sports were in her blood and had even been recruited for college ball but declined. Instead she and Spence married, and Carmen went on to earn her teaching degree at the community college. Carmen slipped into the home dugout and waited. *"What if he didn't show up? What if he showed up but wasn't interested in what she had to say?"* Carmen's thoughts tortured her. As she sat there with her thoughts, she recalled the text she had sent. Immediately, she realized that her phone had a new number! *"What an idiot! Suppose he didn't even know it was her? Suppose he just ignored an unknown number? Should she call him?"* Carmen's heart sunk.

"Dang train! If this county doesn't do something about these stalled crossings, he was going to scream." Flipping through the stations didn't change his situation no more than thumping his steering wheel. With only five minutes to spare, the train engine kicked in gear and forty-eight freight cars rolled on down

the line. Instinctively he turned his Ford F-150 down the little old gravel road so often used in his teenage days. As if it was yesterday, he pulled into the gravel lot right behind the dugouts. He saw her Jeep. He knew she was here. Because it was dark he couldn't tell if she was sitting in her car or not. Parking right beside her, he tried to acclimate his vision to the darkness, but he still could not tell. There were butterflies in his stomach. As hard as it would be, he would fight off the urge to run to her and grab her. He would wait until he knew the purpose of this meeting. No matter her purpose, he wasn't leaving before he said what he had to say, but because she contacted him before he could set his own plan in motion, he would let her go first. *"Deep breaths,"* he thought.

Carmen heard him pull in but because she was enclosed inside the dugout with the back towards the lot, she couldn't yet see him. She was sweating, and it wasn't due to the sweltering heat. Her nerves were shot. *"Could she make things right one more time?"* Carmen inhaled slowly several times willing her heart to slow down.

Spencer scanned the horizon again in search of Carmen. He still didn't see her, so he slowly opened the door and stepped out of his truck. When she heard the knowing creak of his old truck's door, Carmen flipped on the field lights illuminating the infield of the softball diamond. She hadn't known if they would still work but hoped the county had to maintain some lights for security. She had only hoped. Neglected from nonuse and broken poles only half of the bulbs worked but still enough to make known what was to be made known. *"It's now or never!"* she thought.

Startled by the lights suddenly switching on, Spencer blinked to adjust his vision to the brightness. He had just made it around the dugout to the dilapidated fence gate opening to the field. There she was. He gasped. He wanted to giggle, cry and sigh with relief at the sight of her for she was uniformed up in her original high school jersey and visor. As he slowly closed the gap between them, she tossed a glove towards him. He instinctively caught it and flashbacks of their high school days buzzed through his mind.

"Coach says to throw with you"

"I will."

Carmen tosses the ball to Spencer, which he catches and tosses back.

"Coach says you'll help me." She tosses the ball.

"I'll try." He throws the ball back.

"Coach says you'll push me beyond my limits." She throws it back.

"I will do my best." He throws it back.

"Coach says you're pretty good" She throws a little harder.

"Most days" He follows her lead.

"Coach says you're so handsome." She pitched it underhandedly.

"No, she didn't but thank you." He did the same thing.

"Coach says I'm stupid." She held the ball.

"Coach lied." He stood there.

Time stopped. Carmen stared at this man with watery eyes. He was standing twenty feet from her. *"What was making her legs feel like concrete? Why couldn't she move?"*

Carmen willed her legs to work and took two steps. "I'm glad you came."

Spencer took two steps "No other place I'd rather be."

Carmen never took her eyes off his. "Do you remember falling in love on this very field?"

He replied, "I fell in love with you the very first day I saw you." He took a step towards her.

Carmen asked," Do you remember what you asked me the night after my first game?"

Spencer laughed. *"God, she loved his laugh."* "I do. I said, You won the game and you've won my heart. Will you be mine forever?"

Carmen responded, "I still am."

Spencer's heart melted. He closed the gap between them in two giant strides and grabbed her as she leaped into his arms. Time froze. As their bodies merged, the storm clouds opened and cried for them. The pouring rain didn't deter their embrace. It only made their heads separate to look into each other's eyes. The temptation was far too great. Spencer bent down and ever so softly kissed Carmen on the forehead. He then kissed her on the cheek and paused there momentarily. It was Carmen that pressed forward, lifted her head just enough to meet his ripe wet lips with hers. They opened up and kissed deeply and passionately for several minutes before lightning became as intense as their kiss. Spencer reached down and grabbed Carmen's hand and ran through the already puddling mud to the shelter of the dugout. Shaking the excess water out of their hair, they both sat in the dugout. Leaning her head back against the concrete blocks but not letting go of Spencer's hand, she remarked about what a mess she had made.

"Carmen, there's no explanation needed." Spencer interrupted "I read the letter."

"Let me finish, Spence. This is important. Things have changed since I left that letter. I want to explain and then you can make your decision."

Spencer sat back patiently and longingly. He knew from experience that when she needed to get something off her chest, it was best to just sit back and listen.

Carmen recounted every thought and event that happened from the moment she entered the surgery room for the miscarriage. She rehashed all of her thoughts and misguided decisions. These were all memories that she shared with Spencer, yet his interpretation of the feelings was quite different. She paraphrased the letter she had left and how she had been 100% sure that she was doing the right thing. She wanted Spencer to experience fatherhood. Denying him fatherhood would also be denying some children the best dad that would have ever been. She explained how unfair it was for him to never be a daddy. She looked at him with tears in her eyes. "Whether you agree with me or not, do you at least see where I was coming from?"

"I do."

"That leads me to my trip. When I left Georgia, I left you with my heart. I thought I was giving you the only thing I could. I was wandering, Spencer, wandering. I was an empty vessel void

of a heart for it was with you, but somehow in all of that despair,
I found strength. God led me to Carolina. There was where I
found my soul."

"So, that's where you have been?"

"It is"

The next half hour was spent retelling each day in her ram-
shackled cottage, her days in the coastal town and of course her
new friends, Irene and Norman. The tea times and the last day's
conversation were verbalized almost word for word. Again,
Carmen teared up but this time it was Spence that held her hand.
He patiently waited for her to regain her composure. Then she
continued. She reverently finished describing the tattered
leather album and the story her elderly friends recounted for
her.

"I don't want to have blank spaces, Spence. As confident
as I was that I was doing the best thing for you, Irene's story
assured me that maybe I had been wrong. We can lead a full and
happy life without children if that is in God's plan. Irene and
Norman kiss like they are childhood sweethearts still giddy in

love. Norman still brings Irene flowers and takes her out on a date every Sunday after church. Irene said her love for him sixty years later is stronger than it had been when they were newly married. I want that. I have been so engulfed in beating the odds that I have forgotten how to live. I have forgotten how to love you, and I forgot how to let you love me. If you will have me, I will love you for the rest of the days of my life, and I will never ever bring up babies again. I will be content with the fact that you and I are together." Then Carmen sat silent and waited. Her eyes begged for forgiveness.

Spencer knew it was his turn to speak. He knew that Carmen waited for an answer. The story of her summer was just amazing. When he had time, he wanted to revisit that story just to reflect again on the beauty and poignancy of it. Right now, though, he needed some time to digest all that had been revealed. Although it would had been easy to just forgive and forget and pick up where they had left off, he was bound and determined not to deviate from his plan and decision he had derived at after reading her letter. Spencer recalled the precise moment he realized this whole mess had been his fault. He had to correct it.

"Carmen, there's a problem."

Carmen's heart didn't just stop. It literally turned rock solid and crumbled as it made its way to the pit of her stomach. Although Spencer had rehearsed his spill all afternoon long, now the words were difficult to speak. He proceeded to attempt to explain the anguish he had gone through when she vanished. He told her about the long days and even longer nights. He told her of eating outside waiting for her Jeep to come around the curve. He told her of the long walks he took searching for the reasons she left. He told her of the loneliness.

"Carmen, my body ached for you. I got physically sick when I walked through a room and saw something of yours. Our wedding picture, for God's sake still hung over our bed. Do you know how hard that was for me?"

Carmen knew he really didn't want an answer. She just nodded.

"There are no words to describe my emptiness. I asked myself what I had done wrong. What could I have done better? I was a basket case."

"Then came the anger. I felt betrayed. I was royally pissed. I thought we were a team and you didn't even let me play my inning. Yes, I was mad. You made a 100% decision with 50% of the votes. And when you turned your phone off, I was mad all over again. My poor crew took the brunt of my anger. They haven't forgiven me yet."

"Then I felt jealousy. I know that sounds crazy, but I was jealous that somehow you had turned off your emotional radar and just walked away from our marriage without a second thought. To me that is what you had done. I knew that I couldn't do that. I wasn't strong enough. I wished that had I known this was what was going to happen, I had never met you."

Carmen winced. Although she deserved that, it pained her already numb body.

"What you need to remember is up until this time I had not opened the envelope. I didn't know you had left me a letter. I didn't know the reason you left. I only presumed you fell out of love with me. The pain was just so great. A couple of weeks ago, the jealousy of your new life God only knew where just hit me at the wrong time. I called Lance and asked him to take me to numb my pain. I needed to get drunk. So, we did. You gotta understand that night I wanted to forget you if not forever then just for as long as the beer would last. Remembering you and what we had was tearing my insides out. Spencer paused. He knew what was coming. He was at "that part" of the story. Anyway, Lance and I played pool for a while until he ran out of money. He got interested in some girls on the dance floor, I got interested in the ballgame, and a lady at the bar got interested in me."

Spencer glanced at Carmen. He knew that he was about to hurt Carmen, and he would do anything to avoid it. But he couldn't. Realization dawned on Carmen and she thought she might just throw up. She attempted to stand. Spencer took both her shoulders and forcibly made her sit back down. He had never ever been rough with his wife, but this time called for it. She knew he meant business.

"You're going to hear me out. You owe me that."

"At first I tried to ignore her. But the more flirtatious she got and the more beers I had, the easier it became to rationalize that our marriage was already over."

Carmen couldn't hide the tears rolling down her face. Her husband wanted so badly to wipe them away. He turned away to avoid seeing the hurt in her eyes. He knew how deep this betrayal would cut but he had to tell her the whole story.

"Carmen, we danced, and we kissed, and I am so truly sorry."

Carmen waited for the rest. Spencer had to stop himself. Just retelling about this encounter made him sick at his stomach and guilt consumed him. His pause seemed like eternity. Carmen took it to mean end of story. She probably didn't want to hear the rest.

"I shouldn't have come back, Spence. I just got wrapped up in an old person's tale. I'll leave, and we will pretend my conversation didn't happen."

"Dammit, Carmen. Don't you dare do this again. Listen. Let me finish. I could have easily drowned my sorrows that night for a little while. But then I began to feel guilt and shame."

"I didn't want her. I wanted you. We were still married. I ran out of the bar and came home." There was no denying the hurt in his voice for he too shed a tear.

"You didn't make love to her?" Carmen asked.

"Had I left with her it would have never been making love. But no, I left the bar with Lance and came straight home cussing myself the whole way." He couldn't bear to look at her. *"She will never forgive me,"* he thought.

"But I'm glad it happened, Carmen because it slapped me in the face and made me start thinking about us and how I had failed as a husband. When I got home, I found the letter you wrote me. I had never opened the packet until then. When I read your words, I crumbled. What you did for me is nothing short of the most sacrificial gift I have ever heard of. On the flip side, though, it was the most idiotic, stupid, asinine thing I can fathom."

"That's when the shame set in. I cried like a two-year-old baby. I just sat there for hours thinking about our lives and our marriage. I had been so selfish and hadn't even realized it. Although I was shameful of how I acted at the bar, I was more ashamed that I had set up roadblocks and boundaries on an issue you had brought up to me countless times. I never fully allowed myself to consider other options available to us. I never allowed you to ask me. I was selfish. When you lost the baby, I was devastated too. I was devastated because I did want to be a dad but I was also devastated because somewhere during that time I had lost you. So, in fairness I wasn't a team player either. I said no to a question you never directly asked. And there again, you put your desires aside to make me happy. You always do that. Knowing that compounded my guilt times ten."

Carmen was puzzled. She really wasn't sure where he was going with this.

"Carmen, I'm sorry. I'm sorry for everything. Before you texted me today, I had my mind made up that I too was going to a lawyer. However, I was going to a lawyer to initiate procedures for adoption. I was going to bring them to your school when you returned. I knew you would be at school. Although you never point blank asked me, I always changed the subject when you hinted about adopting."

Spencer took a deep breath before finishing.

"Carmen, I promise that if you will come back, I will love you for the rest of the days of my life. So, the problem I mentioned earlier is not me taking you back and hopefully, my stupidity at the bar can be forgiven. The problem is if we get back together that now you don't want children, and I want to adopt. You deserve to be a mommy. I want to be a daddy, and if we can't do it naturally then I will give my whole love to a child that we raise together."

She just leaned her head back on the cold concrete and closed her eyes. The storm raged outside the dugout. Way past dark in the middle of a thunderstorm on a cold hard bench, the answers to life's problems was about to be solved.

Although at one-time Carmen longed to hear Spencer say he would adopt, after Norman and Irene's story she was content with the possibility of living the remainder of her days with her soul mate.

Spencer pondered that perhaps he didn't present his case in the most effective way because Carmen didn't immediately react. *"She won't be able to forgive me about the bar incident. I betrayed her by what happened."* he thought. As difficult as it was, he waited.

Even though he was relieved that he got to see Carmen and relieved that he got all of it off his chest, Spencer was second-guessing the outcome. He convinced himself that he had crossed boundaries unable to be mended.

Carmen shivered. The late nights in Georgia especially after a thunderstorm could turn brisk and cool. Spencer noticed and offered to run to the truck for his blanket. When he returned, he was met by the most content smile he had ever seen. Snuggling Carmen into the blanket, she scooted right next to her husband and laid her head on his shoulders. Happy to be this close, neither of them spoke for quite some time. Both relished in each other's touch and contemplating their next moves.

"Are you sure you want this and not just doing it for me? Cause you know I'll leave again if I think you are sacrificing your happiness" Carmen kidded.

Spencer leaned down to kiss Carmen's nose.

"I'm sure."

With the declaration of solidarity, Carmen and Spencer was a team once more. The light kiss, the lifted weight, the romantic glow of the lightning and the erotic songs of the hooted owl gave way for a feeling of desire.

Spencer lifted Carmen onto his lap and thoroughly explored the taste of her mouth. As she grasped his face with both hands, Carmen straddled this man she had first fell in love with on this field so many years ago as a young girl. Now as a woman, Carmen had fallen in love all over again. Spencer's hands started rubbing up and down her back. When the kisses became more urgent and deep, his hands found her swollen breasts alert and ready for his touch. As he raised her shirt to fully do justice to her mounds of sweetness, he felt his body burn with the need of having her completely. He kissed and tantalized and caressed her upper half. He pressed at the right time and gently massaged as the need arose. Carmen lingered on Spencer's neck. She engulfed him with want and desire kissing up and down his neck as he continued to please her. He moaned with agreement when her tongue found way to his ear. They lingered in this soft phase for a very long time neither ready to hurry it up. Although they both had a burning desire to fulfill their love and consummate their renewed togetherness, they spent quality time where they were.

"It's been too long" Spencer cried. "God, I've missed you."

"I've missed you too," Carmen breathed out. "I want you."

Those words were all it ever took for Spencer. It was time.

"Let's go to my truck," he mumbled, "for old time's sake."

Carmen briefly considered it but opted for something else. As she stood up in front of him, she wiggled her way out of her jeans. She took the blanket that had fallen to the ground and spread it right there before them preparing for she and Spencer to reunite as husband and wife. He gently lowered her softly to the blanket as he too tugged to loosen himself of his jeans. They couldn't tell if minutes or hours had passed as they reacquainted each other with every crevice of their bodies. As rain beat on the tin roof, moans of ecstasy were drowned out. Entering his wife tenderly at first then building to possessively, Spencer reclaimed his wife.

Carmen cried tears of peace.

Just before midnight, Spencer rolled over propping himself on his elbow. He gently swiped a strand of hair from Carmen's eyes and tucked it behind her ear.

"I love you. Tonight was perfect."

"I love you more." Carmen smiled.

"Let's go home. OUR home."

TURQUOISE – THE COLOR OF NEW BEGINNINGS

Chapter 12

Although both were elated beyond imaginable, both were spent. Tired from this journey that had just now ended but excited about new journeys about to begin. Carmen was ready to go home. Spencer was ready for her to be home. As she got back into her Jeep, Spence grabbed the bouquet he bought for her from his truck. He helped her buckle up as he handed her yellow lilies and tulips through her window. He knew which flowers her favorite were as well as her choice in color.

She inside the Jeep and he standing just outside, Spencer whispered, "Thank you."

"See you at home, my love." Carmen put her car in reverse. They both pulled out from the ball field where they first fell in love and have now fell in love all over again.

The ride home wouldn't take long at all. They would be home in less than 15 minutes and life could begin anew. Although the rain had slowed down some, it still required wipers. One thing Carmen loved about Georgia was the constant green of the pines. With the pollen all gone for the season and the rain falling, everything looked fresh even in the middle of the night. Making a permanent move to the Carolinas quickly lost appeal but would always hold a special place in her heart. She wondered if Norman and Irene had ever visited her Georgia. She made a mental note to check in with them in the morning. She added to that note the fact that Spencer might enjoy visiting them over the Thanksgiving holidays. She'd work on that too. It had been many years since she had been down these back roads. She spent a lot of time on these gravel drives throughout high school. She and her friends would park somewhere on one of these pull offs and hike to some old caves. Some said they were haunted. The guys encouraged fear in hopes that the girls would cuddle up to them around the bonfire at the cave. The guys always had a cooler of beer snuck from their parents' cabinets. Spencer was always there as well. He often brought his guitar and strummed it while everyone sat around the fire. Carmen remembers being so proud that he was hers. Even when other girls eyed him with flirtatious batty eyes, Spencer's heart belonged to Carmen. More often than not, the cops would run the kids off sometime near midnight but never really told their parents because they had known each one in the group since they were toddlers. There were a few advantages of living in such a small town. Her mindless reminiscences suddenly stopped short when the only car she had seen tonight came flying around one of the many curves on the rural county road. As a result, when it neared her Jeep, Carmen had to swerve, in turn running off the road. Correcting her slide, she successfully guided her vehicle back between the lines. She glanced in her rearview mirror to make sure Spencer had also evaded that idiot. It was probably some teenager showing out for his girl. His truck lights never wavered and stayed on course several yards behind her. She grinned as she heard him honk at the reckless driver probably in protest of endangering his wife. Spencer has always protected her. It was so easy to lose her train of thought when Carmen daydreamed about him. Without any inkling that something was about to happen, she caught just a slight glimpse of movement to the right. She slowed down a little but just as she entered yet another bend in the road, the deer decided to bolt right out in front of her. Once again, Carmen jerked her Jeep to avoid hitting the deer. Again, she dodged a bullet but about the same time the deer's mate also bolted into the road but became frozen with the oncoming lights of Spencer's truck. Spencer slammed on his brakes but because of the wet slick roads, his slide turned into a long skid right into the apex of the sharp curve. Instantaneously right before striking the deer, Spencer's truck hit the loose gravel on the shoulder of the road and accelerated into a viral spin. Carmen's scream muffled the sounds of glass on asphalt.

Minutes before, Spencer's heart couldn't be more full. What happened tonight had been far greater than what he ever expected. Although a thousand scenarios had played out in his mind, truthfully, he couldn't figure out how the meeting was going to end. Thank God, it went as it did. He replayed the whole night in his head smiling when he thought of Carmen in her softball jersey. That was the way she rolled. She always came up with a creative yet meaningful way to do things. Then he remembered the pain in her eyes when he recounted the bar incident. He knew he had to though; else he wouldn't ever be able to forget it. Although he accepted that she forgave him, he wasn't sure if he ever would forgive himself. Then, completely out of her comfort zone, Carmen led him to the sweetest, most uninhibited, passionate lovemaking he thinks they ever had. Was it because they had been separated so long? Was it because they were not having sex for the sole reason of procreation? Was it because of the realization that love had developed twice at that ball field? No matter, Spencer was still smiling serenely when he witnessed some idiot almost run Carmen off the road. *"Damn teenagers!"* He thought. *"Probably late for curfew."* Spencer should have been in the lead. These back roads can get treacherous at any time but after dark and slick roads compound the danger. Spencer yawned and rubbed his eyes. He just noticed how extremely tired he was. He looked forward to climbing into bed beside his wife and collapsing. Scooting up in his seat and rearranging his hands on the steering wheel, he was focused on getting home. Then, as if in slow motion, Spencer saw the deer at probably the same exact moment as Carmen. He watched her once again swerve to miss the deer that jumped out in front of her. Closely watching Carmen's Jeep to make sure she was safe once again, he never saw the second deer that had also jumped in the middle of the road. Spencer's truck struck the deer, skidded off the shoulder of the road and began a deadly spiral decline down the right-side bank.

Carmen witnessed the accident courtesy of her rear view mirror. Her heart beat accelerated as she tried to simultaneously unbuckle and find her phone to dial 9-1-1. Her pocketbook had fell over and distributed her contents to the floorboard during the first close call. Running to the other side of her Jeep she found it up under the passenger's seat. She saw his truck now turned completely sideways halfway down the ravine creviced between two trees.

"SPENCER!" she cried. No answer. *"Oh, Dear God!"* she thought. She tried to talk to the emergency dispatcher all the while trying to make her way down the steep bank. Although the nice man on the other side of the phone kept telling her to stay on the line, the young wife gave their location said, "Hurry Up!"

and dropped it so that she could use both hands to get leverage to reach Spence.

"I'm coming, baby! Can you hear me?" she kept screaming. The only sounds she heard were spewing of some sort and herself shouting and crying. It was no use trying to maneuver strategically down the bank. The mud and overgrowth made that impossible. She pretty much just slid down tearing her skin and clothes on the way. As she made it to his door, he still wasn't responding to her beckons. She couldn't get the door opened but wasn't sure if it was because of the damage or simply because Spencer had refused to buy a new truck because he was restoring his granddad's old Ford. The door had always been tricky.

"Come on, Baby! You gotta help! We've got to get you out of here! Spence, answer me!"

Using the leverage of the back tailgate and side panels, Carmen half crawled half climbed her way to the passenger's side. This door was easier to open. She climbed in and was stupefied to see her love unnaturally angled only held up with the seatbelt around his waist bleeding from everywhere.

"Oh, God, Spencer" she cried. "Hold on, Help is coming! Hold on baby!"

She didn't know what to do. She always heard moving an injured person may cause more damage than good, but she writhed with the pain he had to be in given that position. As best she could, she moved in and propped his limp body on hers to relieve some of the pressure from hanging there. In the meantime, she was trying to take off her top layer shirt to stop the flow of blood coming from somewhere on his head.

"Oh God, please hurry" Carmen pleaded and begged out loud. "They have got to hurry. Talk to me baby! Can you hear me? Everything is going to be all right. Just hold on, sweetie."

Hours of waiting turned out to be only about eight minutes in real time. Carmen heard the sirens in the distance but dared not move less the weight of Spencer would cause stress again. Thank goodness her Jeep was at the top right where his truck lunged off the road. No doubt, the ambulance would have to see it. Carmen found Spencer's hand and held it and encouraged him to hang on. When she could visibly make out the blue lights above, she frantically started screaming. "We're down here! Hurry, please help!"

Carmen could smell the dried blood on her as she paced the emergency room waiting area. Spencer had lost a lot of blood she knew because she was wearing it. *"This couldn't be happening. This isn't real."* Carmen repeated over and over in her mind. Hadn't they just been in the throes of reunited passion only an hour ago? How could this be? Although there was an abundance of activity here, no doctor or nurse came to discuss her husband's injuries. When she inquired at the desk, they assured her that someone would come get her just as soon as they knew something. She had been allowed to ride in the ambulance with Spence but was quickly ushered to a waiting area when they rushed him back to surgery at the hospital. Now, here she was waiting for some type of news. She didn't have to know the time. It had to be early morning for new faces began appearing with coffee and bagels throughout the ER. *"Must be time for shift change,"* she thought. When she didn't think she could bear it anymore, she headed back up to the information desk for the fiftieth time that night. She almost bumped into a man with a long white coat asking to speak to a Mrs. Simpkins. Carmen hurried her step. "That's me! Is he ok, doctor? What's going on?" Carmen rushed the words.

"Let's step into a private consultation area, ma'am" The doctor replied.

Carmen's world hinged on what he was going to say.

"Mrs. Simpkins your husband sustained some major injuries in the crash. We've cleaned all of the outside wounds, which were ugly but minor. He has a couple of broken ribs plus a fractured collarbone that we can deal with at a later date. The surgery was successful in that we were able to stop the internal bleeding that was coming from his stomach area probably as a result of the broken ribs.

But right now, our major concern is his head injury. Head injuries are tricky; everyone reacts to them differently."

Carmen soaked in as much information as she could all the while trying to process short and long-term solutions. "So, what is the plan? What do we do to fix this?"

"Like I said, Mrs. Simpkins, head injuries are an anomaly. As long as the brain is not bleeding, then our course of action is to just wait. We keep him comfortable and let the brain decide to wake up" the doctor hesitated "or not to wake up".

Carmen raised her head with fury. "You mean there's a chance that?" Carmen's words stopped dead in their tracks. Tears welled behind her eyes yet again.

The doctor patted her knee and affirmed her worst fear. "Pray" he said. "I'll do everything that I can."

"Can I see him?" she asked.

"I'll let you see him only if you will promise that afterwards, you will go home, clean up, eat and rest. He will need you when he wakes up."

Although Carmen wasn't sure she could, she obliged. She followed the white-coated stranger through a maze of corridors and silver-plated doors. She gasped as she walked into the cold sterile room. Spencer, so vivacious hours ago, was hooked up to various machines that were beeping and buzzing. He had tubes coming out of both arms and one very uncomfortable looking one down his throat. She eased up beside his bed, bent down and kissed him on the only space available, his forehead. She willed him to open his eyes both with spoken and unspoken words. She found his hand from underneath the sheet and promised him that everything was going to be ok if he would just open his eyes. "Please open your eyes, Spencer. I need to see your eyes." Spencer's eyes did not open. She stayed in the same position for what seemed like forever before the nurse sympathetically told her that this wasn't a regular room and that she would have to leave periodically so they could do what they needed to do. Carmen didn't have the strength to protest. She kissed Spencer again and told him that she would be back as quickly as possible.

Detached from reality, Carmen headed to the parking lot only to realize she didn't even have a way home. Although there were lots of friends and/or coworkers that she could have called, she just didn't have the energy to explain everything. She called a cab. The driver dropped her off at the sidewalk, and she had to search for inner strength to make her legs walk only a few feet. A few weeks ago, Carmen didn't think she would ever be walking back into this house, and she never dreamed it would be by herself under these circumstances. Carmen dropped her purse on the hall table right inside the front door. She robotically made it to the shower and stood under the hot water until it ran cool. Carmen stepped out and caught a glimpse of herself in the mirror. It was her fault Spencer had that wreck. Number one he was there for her. Number two she had dodged the deer, and he didn't have time to react. Carmen slid down the wall with only her bath towel wrapped around her and sobbed like a baby. She couldn't lose Spence. It had been excruciating enough losing Spence this summer due to her misconstrued separation idea, but actually losing him to death was something she would not survive. Her tears showed no sign of ceasing. The only reconciliation she had was knowing there was a lot to do before getting back to the hospital. Spencer had to know that she was there. Unable to fight the fatigue, she promised herself only to allow time for a short catnap. An hour later, she was suddenly awakened by a knock on the door. Jumping up she knew it was bad news even more so after spotting the police car out front.

"Mrs. Simpkins, we had the tow truck take Mr. Simpkins' truck to the garage but your Jeep has been delivered out back," the young police officer informed her.

Carmen thinks that young man went to her school several years ago but at the moment she couldn't recant anything past yesterday.

Relieved at that news, Carmen just said "Thank you."

"You're welcome, ma'am. I hope everything turns out o.k."

Thankful that the messenger was only there about her vehicles, she hustled around trying to get orientated and goal minded. She made a mental list of all the things she needed to do. Then she made a mental list that every bit of it could wait until she got back to the hospital. She pulled her hair back in a ponytail, threw on some jeans and shirt and raced down the highway back to her Spence.

She halfway sprinted down the hallways and corridors. When she reached the nurse's station on the fourth floor, Carmen asked to be buzzed in. Even though it seemed like it had been an eternity since she had been here, nothing had changed. Spencer lay in the same position with the same monitors and tubes void of life and emotion. His mind still slept.

"I'm here, sweetie. Time to wake up." Carmen coaxed.

Nothing.

Carmen would wait patiently. She would wait until she took her last breath if need be. She again held his hand and talked to him. She told him how hard it was for her going back to their house alone. She told him again how sorry she was for everything and that she was going to make it right.

"Please wake up," she begged.

A sympathetic nurse changing his IV fluids pushed Carmen a chair next to the bed, so she could sit closely to her husband.

There she stayed as long as she could. She knew that sooner or later they would run her off again. But until that moment, she would sit and talk to the love of her life.

During one of her sparse coffee and potty breaks, Carmen dialed Irene to update her on the news. She still wasn't in the mood to talk but felt obligated to let her elderly friend know what had transpired. Oddly, Irene comforted Carmen even through the cellular phone waves. She still couldn't fathom how her friend always had just the right words of encouragement to get her through one more trial and tribulation.

With a renewed and refreshed sense of purpose, Carmen made some written notes of everything she needed to do and people that should be contacted. She also put them in order of priority. She laughed. Spencer always poked fun of her for being so goal orientated. As she sat beside the hospital bed, Carmen offered up silent prayers. She willed herself to believe that he was just asleep and being difficult to wake up like so many Saturday mornings in their little house. She dared negative thoughts to come in her mind and when they did, she changed positions or got up and walked around to the other side of the bed. She often looked out the window and thought back to the day after her miscarriage when she and Spence left this very hospital. Carmen prayed that this too would eventually be a bad memory.

Minutes turned into hours. Hours turned into days. Carmen became familiar with the different nurses and doctors on each shift as well as the differences in protocol. Every update with the doctor was the same. No changes.

The hospital social worker visited with her often and gave her pamphlets about brain traumas. She said to expect the worst and hope for the best. She emphasized the importance of carrying on a normal routine. Carmen bucked anything short of sitting here all day every day but even while doing so, she knew the social worker was right. Carmen had already missed the first several days of teacher preparation. Although the administrators were sympathetic, Carmen knew it wasn't fair to her students to have a substitute during the first few weeks of school. She loved her job and wanted the best for every single child assigned to her each year. The nurses agreed to call at a moment's notice if there were changes. Once again, Carmen pulled her grandmother's phrase to mind. *"Get your big girl panties on."* So, she did. She settled into an energy draining routine. She taught her fifth graders each day with a false pretense that everything was hunky dory. She dashed to the hospital immediately when the 3:00 school bell rung. Her co-workers were all great friends and made her life so much easier. They made most of the lesson plans and picked up every single extra duty that they could so that Carmen could split as soon as possible every day. They carried her load and lovingly listened to her on days when Carmen needed to talk and left her alone when they knew that a hug or an inquiring question would cause her to bust out in tears. Being a teacher requires somewhat of a façade, and she knew that losing it emotionally in front of 25 ten-year olds wouldn't be a good thing. She got pretty efficient at multi-tasking between everything that tugged at her heart. The few hours that she stayed at the hospital each night were spent telling Spencer of her day's activities and continuously begging him to wake up.

She would stay at the hospital until the night shift nurses did their nightly check in. One particular nurse became a personal favorite and somewhat of a confidante. Her name was Kimm. Carmen would make the drive home each night making mental notes of her "to do list" for the next day. Sometimes Carmen would grab a bite to eat, but most nights she just showered and collapsed into bed. Saturday mornings were spent sorting the mail and paying bills. She generally made it back to her second home by noon. She loved Saturdays because after they had moved Spencer to a regular room and out of ICU, Carmen got to bathe her husband on Saturdays. The bath really only consisted of rubbing dry shampoo into his hair and shaving his weeklong growth on his face. Still, Carmen felt honored to take care of him the only way she knew how. She then used hand towels wet with a bedpan of water on the hospital bed to wash and massage each part of his body.

"You're clean now, Spence. You're ready for a date. Wake up baby, let's go on a date." There was still no response.

Sundays were just another Saturday minus the bill paying. The hospital offered a small church service on the same floor Spence was on, so she tried to make time for that as well. She also always checked in with Irene and Norman on Sundays. She waited until after their date time though not wanting to interrupt their "loving time" as Norman called it. Irene always had words of love and encouragement and never failed to make Carmen feel optimistic. Carmen loved that sweet woman. But on the last phone call Sunday, Irene expressed concern.

"Dear, you don't sound like yourself."

"I'm fine. I'm just ready for Spence to wake up."

Irene accepted what she said as truth, but after she hung up, she knelt down in prayer for her young mentee knowing the hurt she felt in her heart.

Life became a series of routines. Carmen settled into this life of routines. She was in it for the long haul. If the X-rays and CAT scans showed brain activity like the doctors said, then he should eventually wake up. They also forewarned Carmen that the longer he stayed unconscious, the greater possibility of damage to his mind if he did become conscious. They cautioned her that he might have some serious mental and physical issues when he woke up, and they still always followed their conversations with "if he wakes up." Carmen despised those words. She was really getting anxious for this nightmare to be over.

Although Spencer looked like Spencer, Carmen could tell that he was withering away. His eyes were sunk in and when she held his hand, she noticed his once rugged calloused hand had turned into brittle bones with very loose skin. His color seemed paler. She could see the frailness in his lifeless body. He looked like a prisoner of war, and Carmen's heart hurt.

This journey was taking a toll on Carmen as well. She hadn't noticed. She hadn't cared, but it became very obvious when she started falling asleep every afternoon at the hospital. Several times while propped up on the bed rails, a nurse would gently pat her on the back and tell her it was "closing time." One afternoon, Kimm shoved a subway sandwich in Carmen's face and told her to eat it.

"Y'all have been here how long, Carmen?"

Carmen had the days inscribed in her mind. "Thirty-five days."

"Thirty-five days since Spencer talked to me." Although not as long as the time spent apart during the summer, thirty-five days in this situation seemed like eternity. What she would do to just hear Spencer speak her name, open his eyes, smile or even just flinch in pain. Something... anything.

"Not one time since I've been his nurse have I seen you eat."

Kimm had become more than a nurse. She was Carmen's friend. The nurse was right. Short of school lunches and vending machine crackers, Carmen couldn't remember a solid sit-down meal.

The two women ate together. Kimm also prayed with Carmen each night before heading home. Then the cycle would restart. This new life was a series of cycles, gut wrenching cycles.

Carmen felt like she was taking advantage of her coworkers, but they continually carried the burden minus classroom instruction well up to close to Christmas break. On one hand she welcomed the approaching holidays because she was barely staying above water trying to keep up with everything. She was only functioning. She needed a break. A few days off work would ease the difficult routine. On the other hand, she dreaded spending Christmas day without their normal traditions and activities. When she discussed her sadness about this to Irene, Irene as always had words of wisdom that spoke straight to her young friend's soul.

"Carmen, these are just moments in that photo album, moments that ya'll are together. Talk to his heart and hold on baby. As difficult as it may be, honey, take pictures. These are the moments, yours and Spencer's moments. No blank spaces."

Carmen vowed to make this Christmas as special as any other Christmas they had spent together. She made several notes about what all needed to be done during the last week of school. The week before a holiday was always crazy at an elementary school. Carmen made every effort to stay jolly and positive during class while maintaining some type of order in her chaotic room.

She left the last day of school before winter break more tired than she had been in a while. In fact, for the first time since the accident, Carmen almost went home for a nap before visiting Spencer. The combination of all the cookies and candy and excitement of the day was not settling well on her stomach either. Knowing that Spencer was lying in a bed fighting for his life caused her to feel shameful and rather than turning right to head home out of school, she instinctively turned left headed for the hospital.

GRAY – THE COLOR OF DESPAIR

Chapter 13

Due to traffic and parking issues, Carmen was running a little late. Kimm was already waiting for her in room 4015. It had become customary that Kimm brought Subway sandwiches on Friday for the two. That was their time.

"Girl, you look worn out. Tell you what, after supper tonight you have ten minutes with your man. Then I'm personally escorting you to your car and you're going HOME to sleep until Sunday."

"I'll be alright. My kids were just overly active today. A class full of ten-year olds high on sugar and Christmas cookies makes for one tired teacher. I'm just pooped."

They laughed.

Kimm pulled the rolling hospital tray over between them and began pulling out sandwiches and chips.

"Tuna salad, my dear. Your favorite."

"No candles?" Carmen teased.

"Turkey and roast beef for myself, my usual."

149

As Carmen took her first bite, she noticed blinking lights going crazy on Spencer's monitor. That had never happened. Simultaneously, the room started spinning and the smell hit her like a rotten egg had been stuffed up her nose. Then the room went black."

Kimm didn't make it to her friend before she hit the ground. She punched Spencer's emergency button on his call box and yelled for help knocking their entire supper to the floor in the process.

Carmen's vision reemerged fuzzy at first and then blindly clear. She knew this place. She was once again looking up at the super magnified lights inside an emergency room just above a patient gurney. She laid on top of that patient gurney.

Kimm's strawberry blond hair and freckled face popped into her the space right above Carmen's nose. "What's going on?" Carmen mumbled.

"Girl, I'm a nurse but you pulled one on me. Fainted right then and there and made me drop my sandwich. You owe me a new one."

Carmen grinned but the pounding in her head prevented her from responding.

"I knew I ate too much divinity at the school party today. My stomach was a little tore up on my way up here. I'll be fine."

The doctor walked around into Carmen's peripheral vision as well. It was the same doctor that treated Spencer the night of the accident. Despite the bad news he gave her that night, he was honest and kind. Carmen liked him.

"Maybe so, Mrs. Simpkins but acute and total physical exhaustion didn't help any either. Your body is dehydrated and exhausted. It is imperative that you take care of yourself. You are no good to Spencer frail and fainting."

"I understand, doctor. I'm honestly trying to do the best I can."

"That's just not good enough, ma'am. How far along are you?"

"Do what? What do you mean how far along am I?"

The doctor looked just as confused as Carmen. "Well your preliminary blood tests showed high pregnancy hormones present in your system. We didn't do a physical exam, of course, because we assumed you knew.

Carmen froze. In fact, it took Kimm putting her arms around her that shook reality into the examination room. Carmen thought she might just faint again. In fact, she did. Again, Kimm stood over her demanding that she wake up.

Once again, the patient regained clarity and demanded to be released. "Kimm you have got to make them do the blood tests over again. I can't get pregnant. I'm sure it is a mistake." Jokingly she added, "Maybe one of my kids food poisoned me." Carmen mentally thought back calculating the last time she had even taken her clomid. It was well before her miscarriage attesting to the fact that she was not pregnant. Mother Nature had once again played a cruel joke. There was just no way she was with child.

"Carmen, I was in here when they drew your blood, but if it will make you feel better, I'll see what I can do."

"I need to get back to Spencer."

"You're gonna go tell him goodbye and go home. Doctor's orders."

Although her mind fought the idea of leaving early tonight, her body was betraying her by rumbling and attempting to spew up the few bites of tuna sandwich that Kimm had brought her. Carmen was certain the queasiness had to do with either the fishy sandwich or the sugar overload from the kid's Christmas party.

Carmen's phone double buzzed signaling a text.

Come quick – Spencer is awake.

Carmen thought she would faint again and when the room spun and started getting fuzzy again, Kimm sensed the urgency, put her in a wheelchair and raced back up to the fourth floor. *"There were some perks of working here. "* Kimm thought. As they waited for the elevator door to open, Carmen remembered the new beeping lights that started flashing just as her world began to spin.

Carmen lifted herself out of the stupid wheelchair before entering Spencer's room. No way in this world would his first sight of her be in a wheelchair. *"Suck it up,"* she thought. Her heart beat with anticipation. *"Thank you, God. Thank you, God!"*

It took only two large strides to make it to Spencer. The headboard of the bed had already been raised to a sitting position. His eyes were still closed though. *"They said he was awake! Had I missed it?"*

"Spencer – I'm here baby. Can you look at me?"

Slowly, Carmen could see Spencer struggle to turn his head towards her voice and ever so slowly raise his eyelids just enough that Carmen could see the whites of his eyes.

Putting one hand on his chest and one hand over her mouth in shock, Carmen pleaded for him to keep on. "Open both of them, baby, all the way. Look at me. I'm here. Come on. You can do this."

With great difficulty, Spencer obeyed. Carmen kissed his face, and on cue the well within her soul erupted into volcanic size tears of relief.

"sltoltpppp, o ore jearrrsss." Spencer mumbled.

Carmen's heart soared. "What was that, baby. Say it again."

Spencer carefully ordered his words to come out right. Slowly but precisely, he spoke.

"Stop. No more tears." As plain as day, Spencer had just told her to stop crying. She had no other choice but to laugh and obey.

The doctors came in and did their full body examination complete with mini physical tests to see if Spencer's mind comprehended commands. For the most part, he was slow but succeeded in performing the physical actions.

"This is an excellent sign" the doctor commented. "In the morning, we will do a battery of new CAT Scans and MRIs to see what has developed. Until then take it easy and enjoy looking at your pretty wife." The doctor patted his patient on the hand and left.

Spencer knew that was an easy promise to keep. Despite the rules, Carmen crawled right up in bed with Spence and spent the night looking into his eyes and listening to his heart. Despite the sore collarbone, painstakingly, he even lifted his arm to wipe away a tear that leaked from her eye.

"I'm not crying because I'm sad, Spence. I'm crying because this is the best day of my life. I'm happy."

Although they both drifted off sometime in the wee hours of the night, Carmen never felt Spence's arm come unwrapped from around her shoulders. Only the six a.m. medicine delivery disturbed the two. The room became a buzz of nurses taking blood, changing IVs and hospital volunteers delivering breakfasts. Two orderlies filed in soon after into the already crowded room. They had orders to take Spencer to the fifth floor. They assured her that he would be gone for several hours for blood work, imaging scans and then a complete physical rehabilitation evaluation. He mouthed "I love you" as she leaned down to kiss him. She felt safe to run home and do some errands including call Irene and even get Spencer some clothes he would need. *"Spencer's going to need some clothes to come home in."* That made her smile. Butterflies danced in her gut. On the drive home, she realized that she had not eaten since the night before and that embarrassing fainting spell, so she added a drive through stop to her route. Although Carmen was queasy with giddiness, she completed all of her chores in record time and was in the room waiting when they rolled Spencer back.

Weak but ecstatic, Spencer beamed, "just got a clean bill of health. I'm healthy as a horse."

"I don't think he's as strong as a horse yet, but it's true. All the tests showed full function of his brain. You must have had an open line to the big guy up above."

The doctor even discussed releasing him after twenty-four more hours of observation. "That is if you behave," Kimm teased.

PURPLE – THE COLOR OF HEALING

Chapter 14

Thank God it was Christmas break. That meant Carmen had two weeks to get Spencer settled at home, rest and then concentrate on rebuilding their lives.

"Would you quit fussing over me, babe," Spencer protested. "You heard the doctor. I'm as good as new."

"I'm not taking any chances, and you're not quite as good as new. You got taped up ribs and a plastic thingy-ma-jig on your shoulders."

"Technicalities, babe, technicalities. And as much as I like having you by my side, you don't have to help me walk. I'm fine. In fact, I don't want to be cooped up any longer. Let's go for a walk. Better yet, let's take off. I want to meet your Irene and Norman. You know, I feel like I owe them my marriage." Spencer gently kissed the top of Carmen's head. She heard a little moan of discomfort escape him as he bent.

"I don't think that is a good idea quite yet. I don't want to get you too far away from your doctors just in case. Besides, I don't want to share you with anyone for a long long time." She

teased.

Spencer reluctantly agreed if nothing else but to assure

his wife that he had in fact made almost a complete recovery.

The tension and stress must have taken its toll on Carmen more

than she realized. Although she was finally at complete peace

with everything, her body just couldn't get enough rest. She

rationalized it because it had indeed been an intense few

months. But, it was almost all she could do to cook Spencer's

favorite dinner that night and that was the one thing she

promised. He said no man should ever have to live off of liquid

nutrients through an IV like he had for the last twenty-one

weeks. He jokingly ribbed Carmen that any good wife would

have pureed a rare rib eye steak to feed him through that bag.

Still, Carmen couldn't shake the exhaustion she felt. "*I need to get

back on my vitamin regiment,*" she thought. "*That will perk me

up.*" While the chicken pot pie baked in the oven, she slipped off

down the hall. In the bathroom, she searched everywhere for her

multi vitamin that she had so religiously taken before her

summer departure. She made a mental note to pick some up the next time she was out. When she pulled open the drawer that normally kept her extra bottles, Carmen's gasped. The sight of the feminine products brought back the fainting incident the night Spencer woke up. She had completely blocked it from her recollection. She had been so preoccupied with Spencer's recovery and getting him home, she completely forgot. *"Could it be? Do I want to even get my hopes up?"* Carmen braced herself on the sink and realized in fact that she hadn't had a period since she got back from Carolina. She never had the time to even think about it. She had barely managed to just get by with all that had happened. Surely the chances of having sex only one time, the night at the ball field, wouldn't be good enough to change the course that she and Spencer had been on for years. She convinced herself she was crazy and vowed to not slip into that same pattern that had consumed her in the past. *"New beginnings,"* she thought. She closed the bathroom drawer forgetting it once again.

On her way back to the kitchen, she heard the doorbell ringing. That had to be some of Spencer's crew. They had asked to come by for a brief visit. Spencer said they just needed him to come back to work because he always bought lunch on Fridays. Carmen laughed at how guys showed affection. Unlike women, they punched and ribbed and teased the people they liked most. When she opened the door, however, it was Kimm. Hugging her friend, she was pleasantly surprised to see her.

"Thank you for coming by, come let me repay you for all of the Subways you bought me. I have homemade chicken pot pie in the oven."

"Girl, don't tempt me. I would love to, but I don't have time. I'm on company business."

"The doctor sent you to make a house call on Spence?" Carmen quizzed. "Now that's old school."

"Nope, this time it's for you, sweetie." Kimm's eyes were compassionate and tender as she handed Carmen a small envelope.

Instinctively, Carmen knew what it was but slowly opened it to make sure.

Carmen Simpkins: Positive Blood Test – Confirmed

Pregnancy.

BLUE – THE COLOR OF CONFUSION

Chapter 15

A few months later, she received a message from the front office to call someone named Norman. The number, however, wasn't the number at their store. A sinking feeling came over her. She had already told herself to check in with Irene after school. Today was the last day of a very trying school year. This summer was going to be way different than last. This year, she would be making a planned trip back to Carolina. She had been planning this surprise ever since Spencer had mentioned it the first day he came home from the hospital. That had been Christmas last year. The Christmas she had dreaded turned out to be the best one ever. She had been given the best gift of all time. Completely healed and raring to go, Spencer waited outside on Carmen. Carmen vowed to not miss any more school days than necessary, so they were going to hit the road just as soon as she could tie up all loose ends at work. Irene and Norman didn't know they were coming, so why was Norman calling? She pulled out her cell phone, dialed the strange number and waited for her favorite crotchedy old man to pick up.

"Sea Grove Memorial Hospital. May I help you?" Carmen wondered if she had misdialed for it was a young woman's voice on the other end.

"Uh, I think I got the wrong number. I'm looking for a Norman Coleman."

"Please hold. I'll check."

Carmen's mind began to race.

"Ma'am. There is no Norman Coleman here. We do have a Irene Coleman. Would you like for me to transfer you?"

The wind was knocked out of Carmen once again. "Yes, please."

Sick to her stomach, she waited.

Norman picked up. "Hello, is this Carmen?" He never wasted words.

"Norm, what's going on? What's wrong?" Carmen yelled into the phone for she knew he was deaf in one ear and hard to hear in the other.

"Sweetie, it's Irene. Please come. She's asking for you."

Carmen dropped the phone and jumped in the passenger seat and ordered Spencer to kick it. As so many times in the past year, the wind was knocked out of her emotional gut.

They made the journey in record time despite the mandatory stops that just couldn't be avoided. It was way into the night before they pulled into the parking lot.

"Man, she was tired of hospitals." Whispering prayers for her dear friend, they located Irene's room with ease.

"Do you want me to wait in the hallway?" Spencer asked.

"Just for a bit. Let me speak with Norman first."

Carmen quietly tip toed in not to disturb Norman if he was trying to sleep. Observing from the half-opened door, Carmen's eyes welled up. It was as if she was in the story Irene told her about from many years ago. Norm was at his wife's bedside stroking her hair, holding her hand and willing her to hold on. She didn't know how long Irene had been here. She had talked to her just last Sunday on their weekly telephone call. It had to be around 4:00 because Carmen always waited until after Irene and Norman's date. No matter, Irene was here, and Norm was here. Because it was after visiting hours, Carmen was one hundred percent sure that Norm had likely busted his way into this hospital room like he did in the birthing room. She was equally sure that he had never left his sweetheart's side. He was the most perfect stereotypical example of a true gentleman that she knew. Carmen walked up and placed her hand on Norman's shoulder. He never looked up for he knew who it was.

"I'm sorry I scared you, sweetie. I knew you'd come."

"No place I'd rather be. What's happened, Norman?"

With more effort than required last summer, Carmen noted, Norman stood. "Irene, my dear, wake up. Wake up. Your girl is here."

"Norm, let her sleep. I will be here tomorrow."

Norman finally turned to hug his self-proclaimed god granddaughter. He insisted. "Sweetie, you don't understand. My love is barely hanging on. She has been waiting for you. It's time." Carmen felt the urgency and pivotal air in the room.

Irene roused enough for recognition to show on her face. Carmen held her hand on one side of the bed while Norman, true to character, stayed on the other side of his dying wife.

Carmen felt the dire urgency in the hospital room. She squeezed her friend's hand and kissed her forehead. "Irene, I'm here. Time to go home and have our tea and cake."

"She probably won't respond except with her eyes and facial expressions. Her sweet voice left me yesterday. Haven't heard a peep out of her. " Norm whispered.

Carmen quickly updated her on life and attempted to express how much her friendship meant to her in words. She wasn't doing a very good job with it. Words just hung in her throat. Subtly, Irene squeezed her hand back as if assuring her young friend that it was reciprocated. "At least she knows I'm here," Carmen cried.

"Oh, she knows," Norman assured.

"I want to show you something, Irene. I have someone I want you to meet."

Carmen waved for Spencer to enter the tiny little hospital room. Spencer had overheard the conversation from the hallway. She never ceased to amaze him. He only hoped that he would be as stoic and passionate as she was in times of need. And Norman, Carmen had described him to a "t". He had never met the man in person but felt like he knew him. He couldn't wait to shake his hand. *"First things first though,"* he thought.

Spencer quietly walked into the dimly lit room holding his precious little angel in the crook of his arm. As he reached Irene's bedside, Carmen lovingly took the baby and laid her on Irene's chest.

"Irene, I'd like to introduce you to our daughter, Darcy Irene Simpkins."

Everyone in the room wept.

PINK – THE COLOR OF LOVE

ACKNOWLEDGEMENTS

Everyone has a road to travel. Although this is a work of fiction, it is based on several events in my life. Which ones? I won't tell you. I'll leave that up to your imagination. However, a story as deep as this one couldn't be written without having a relationship with some of these "Spencers" "Irenes" or "Kimms". Thank God that I've been blessed by knowing some precious people throughout the years. I hope the road you travel is full of both painful and wonderful memories. It is those painful memories that helps make the wonderful ones so much more wonderful. Embrace the day; we are not promised tomorrow.

Meet the Author

Dr. Carol Thompson is a public school media specialist in the town where she grew up. She received her doctorate degree in 2009 after writing her dissertation on the topic of bibliotherapy- using books to cope with the stress of everyday life.

She is the author of the Mr. Wiggle series for children as well as other children's and professional books. *Red: The Color of Failure* is her first adult novel. She also writes for various magazines. She can be found on Facebook – Carol Thompson Author.

In her spare time, she loves to travel with her family and scrapbook the memories she collects. She lives with her husband, two children, and two spoiled dogs.

Made in the USA
Lexington, KY
01 August 2018